My Tudor Queen

My Story.

My
Tudor Queen

The Diary of

Eva De Puebla, London 1501-1513

by Alison Prince

While the events described and some of the characters in this book may
be based on actual historical events and real people, Eva De Puebla is a
fictional character, created by the author, and her diary is a work of fiction.

This edition produced for the Book People Ltd,
Hall Wood Avenue, Haydock, St Helens WA11 9UL

First published in the UK by Scholastic Ltd, 2001

ISBN 0 439 95493 2

Typeset by TW Typesetting, Midsomer Norton, Somerset
Printed and bound by Nørhaven Paperback A/S, Denmark
Cover image: Self portrait, 1559-61 by Sofonisba Anguisciola (1527-1625)
Pinacoteca di Brera, Milan, Italy/Bridgeman Art Library

London, England
1501

4th November 1501

I hardly like to make a mark on the beautiful, blank pages of this book, but I must. Mama gave it to me as a parting present so that I could write about this journey from Spain to England. "Don't waste it," she said. "Just write the important things. The big ones."

That was three months ago. It was August when we sailed from Corunna – but how could I write in that terrible storm? We had hardly been at sea for two days when it struck us. People were weeping and praying and being thrown about like dried peas in a baby's rattle. One of our ships sank. I came up to get some air because the smell below decks was so awful, and I saw her roll over helpless as a dead thing, and then the towering waves swallowed her. We were driven back to the Basque coast, with broken masts and rigging washed overboard, and it was a month before the repairs were done and we could start out again. Even then, we were tempest-tossed, but at last we landed in Plymouth.

People came aboard to meet us, and Catherine received them with truly royal dignity. Although she is my childhood friend, I have always known she was a princess – but until that day, I hadn't realized how perfectly she can play the part. The English were delighted with her, and seemed impressed that she asked to go to a church to give thanks for our safe arrival, even before we could change our clothes or have something to eat. She is not yet sixteen but she has great self-possession.

Would Mama think these were big things? I'm sure she would be impressed by the great procession in which we have slowly made our way from the West Country to London. Horses and carriages, litters and baggage-waggons and attendants, soldiers, courtiers, ladies, pages, jesters – and Catherine herself, Catherine of Aragon, on her way to wed Prince Arthur, eldest son of the King of England.

But there have been little things as well, yellow leaves on the trees that stand everywhere, and skies full of birdsong. Grass and tall weeds, rain and mud. Oh, the mud! Mama warned me that England was a wet place, but I never imagined such mud. Perhaps it will be better in London, but so far the journey has been heavy going. The horses have floundered knee-deep sometimes, struggling to get a foothold, and the carriages lurch and splash, and sometimes we have had to stop because of a broken axle or lost wheel. We've all been grateful for an occasional dry day of autumn sunshine.

I have been wretchedly homesick sometimes, longing for warmth and the smell of Spanish cooking. And Mama. When will I see her again? But at least Uncle Rodrigo is in London. When I was small, I used to call him Uncle Rod, but Mama warned me not to use that pet name in front of the courtiers. To them he is Doctor Rodrigo Gonsalez De Puebla, ambassador to England from Catherine's parents, King Ferdinand and Queen Isabella of Spain. He has a son whom I have never met, called Gonsalvo, so at least I will have some sort of family in this strange land.

Tonight we are lodged at the manor house of some lord, not far from London. It is cold in this room although a smoky fire burns in the hearth. The candle flame gutters in the wind that blows in through the glassless windows. Our windows in Spain are not glazed, either, but it is different for us. Wrought-iron grilles keep thieves out and let in whatever air there is to cool our sun-hot walls and floors. These English are a mystery to me. How do they endure the cold? It is dirty, too. The floors are strewn with rushes, fresh ones being scattered over the filth and dropped food of

9

the previous day, and although the dishes are of gold or silver plate, the noblemen do not always bother to go outside or to the retiring room when they need to relieve themselves. They behave, it seems to me, very much as the dogs do which skulk round the tables and snatch at thrown scraps of meat.

Perhaps it is as well that I write my diary in Spanish! It has a hasp and lock on its leather cover, too, so it is safe, I hope, from prying eyes. I could equally well write in English if I chose. That is why I am here, for my skill as an interpreter. The Queen would not have sent me simply as Catherine's childhood friend, or because we share a love of embroidery. Mama is the chief embroideress at the Spanish court, and is necessarily quite close to the Queen, but Isabella has no use for sentiment, except when it comes to the passion she feels for her religion. "Isabella the Catholic", they call her, perhaps in fear as much as in admiration. When Catherine and I were small, she rode against the Moors in full armour at the head of her troops, and she will tolerate no wavering from what she considers the true Church.

These things are not for me to comment on. My place here has nothing to do with embroidery or friendship, though both of these will be useful. I serve as Catherine's interpreter, and stand close by her when the important and gorgeously dressed nobles present themselves, murmuring the meaning of what they say so that only she can hear. That way, at least she can smile or look grave as is suitable, and trot out her few English phrases in the right place. "Yes … no … thank you." Poor Catherine.

What am I saying? How absurd to call her poor when she is a princess of Castile, her mother's youngest and favourite daughter! Yet I do pity her, somehow. She seems so young, though she is only six months behind me, her birthday on December 16th, mine on the tenth day of June. We look very different, though. She is all honey and cream, with skin the colour of a just-ripening peach, while I am as dark as an olive. Papa was a scholar and teacher, and I take after him in many ways. I still miss him, though it is three years since he died. I inherited his bookishness and love of learning – though nothing else, for he was never a rich man – and I think the Queen considered me a good influence on her frivolous-minded daughter.

Catherine always wanted to be active, and lessons bored her. She would sit pouting over her Latin grammar (though goodness knows Latin is easy enough, being so close to Spanish), twisting a strand of her honey-gold hair round her finger, and if voices sounded from the courtyard below she would jump up at once to see who it was, and then laugh and wave from the window. She should have been a boy, I think. She was much happier with the practical subjects which her mother insisted on, riding and shooting, falconry and archery. She even quite liked the domestic skills of baking and weaving and spinning. And she loves embroidery. My mother taught us our needlework. We used to sit outside sometimes, in the shade of the feathery pepper trees, stitching our designs of leaves and tendrils and curving arabesques while we chattered of whatever we fancied.

Mostly, we used only one colour – black or dark red – which stood out on the white cloth, but from what I have seen here, the English delight in a riot of scarlets and purples, blues and gold. I think they see things differently. In the burning sun of Spain, one sees through eyes half-shut against the glare. Things are silhouetted: the curls of wrought iron, the intricate droop of the acacia tree. One never need narrow the eyes here. The light is gentle, the colours a constant shifting of greens, blues and greys highlighted by bright berries and sky-reflecting water.

These are little things – Mama would scold me. The candle is almost burned down, I must go to bed.

5th November 1501

We have come to a place called Dogmersfield, and hardly had we entered the house when in rushed a Spanish ambassador – not my uncle, but a man called Don Pedro de Ayala – to warn us that the King himself was outside, demanding to meet with Catherine.

Doña Elvira was horrified. She is Catherine's duenna (a sort of governess), ferocious at the best of times – and this was not the best. Poor thing, she is bruised black and blue from being jolted about in a carriage. I'm so glad I'm young enough to ride! Anyway, Doña Elvira heaved herself to her feet and went out grumbling, and we heard her protests being translated for the King. "No, Your Majesty, it is not possible to see the princess. It is not the custom for a bride to be seen by the groom or his father before the wedding day." It was a polite translation – her Spanish was a lot more forthright. Don Pedro explained that the princess was resting, but the King cut in, "I don't care if she's in her bed asleep. I am coming in to see her."

Doña Elvira came back with her face as red as a peony – she is not used to being argued with. And behind her came King Henry himself – King Henry VII of England – a lean, determined man with a mouth set like a trap.

Catherine was not in the least flustered. She swept him a low curtsey, and his rat-trap mouth relaxed into a smile as he kissed her hand then stood back to look at her. Carefully, he noted her trim figure and the dancer's grace with which she stands and moves, her small hands and feet, her creamy skin and clear grey eyes. His own eyes ran down the long flow of her honey-coloured hair and his smile broadened. He looked, I thought, like a horse trader, well-pleased by the thoroughbred filly he has bought.

He and Catherine conversed (if one can call it that) in Latin, neither of them knowing a word of the other's language, and Doña Elvira stood with folded arms and a thunderous face. Half an hour later, Prince Arthur himself arrived with a large entourage, and he, too, came in to inspect his bride.

Catherine looked at him, then carefully avoided meeting my gaze. I knew why. Arthur, at fourteen, is a slender boy, little more than a child. He has great charm and sweetness, but his shoulders are narrow and any emotion brings a blush to his pale cheeks. He is as tall as Catherine, but looks much less strong. Everyone was scrupulously courteous, and if Catherine is disappointed, she will never, ever say so.

7th November 1501

Tonight we are in the city of London, lodged at the Bishop's Palace. There is glass in the windows here, for which I am grateful.

We were escorted into the city by a great cohort of the Duke of Buckingham's men. They were dressed in scarlet and black so that they looked like glowing coals, and the long red banners above them flickered like flames. And at St George's Fields we all came to a halt, for another troop of men was approaching. And at their head rode young Henry Tudor, brother of Prince Arthur, sent by his father to greet us.

What a boy! Only ten years old, but already as tall as his older brother, and far stronger and more confident. He swung himself from his horse, tossed the reins to a servant whom he did not even look at, then advanced towards us with a smile on his handsome face, doffed his feathered cap and bowed low. One of our ladies murmured quietly in Spanish, "A pity this boy is not the elder." Several of the others nodded and Catherine, curtseying to young Harry, as they call him, looked up to meet his gaze and could not look away.

Shivers ran down my back. In that moment, the pair of them seemed to belong together, young though Prince Harry is – but of course, the children of royalty are not free to follow the wishes of their hearts. In just a week from now, Catherine will marry the older brother, Arthur, and nothing will alter that.

Evidently the people of London are all set for a great fiesta. Flags and banners fly everywhere, and fantastic arches have been built across the streets, painted to look like bridges or castles, and wherever I look there are elaborate designs that link the arms of England with the crimson pomegranate of Granada. It's all very exciting – and I'm so proud of Uncle Rod. I know from his letters to Mama, who is his niece, how hard he has worked for many years to bring about this marriage between England and Spain. I look forward so much to seeing him.

9th November 1501

At last! Uncle Rod came to the Bishop's Palace today. He is much older than I remember him, and somehow not as big. I used to think he was a tall man, but I suppose that was because I was only small. He is barely my height now, and rather dumpy in shape, with his coat buttons not quite meeting across his tummy. Properly speaking, he is my *great* uncle, of course, but I had never thought of that before. His son, Gonsalvo, came as well, a dark-haired man much older than me, together with his wife, Bianca, and their baby son, Miguel. Gonsalvo is a lawyer, like Uncle Rod, but he shook his head when I asked if he was at court, and said he would rather deal with the rogues of the street than such a parcel of monkeys. Uncle Rod frowned at him and told me to take no notice.

Both of them are much annoyed that Don Pedro de Ayala has come to London. His job was supposed to be in Scotland, arranging a marriage between the Scottish king, James IV, and another of King Henry's children, Princess Margaret. Gonsalvo says Don

Pedro probably finds it more comfortable here than in the rough, cold court of Scotland. Can it really be colder than it is here? I tremble to think of it.

12th November 1501

People stare at us wherever we go. I suppose it is because we look different from the tall, pale English. I heard a man murmur to his companion that we looked like "pigmei Ethiopes". He spoke in Latin, but did he imagine we were too uncivilized to understand? "Pygmy Ethiopians" indeed! How rude! I asked who the man was, and learned that his name is Thomas More. It makes me wonder what the King, for all his courtesies, really thinks of us.

We met Prince Arthur's sisters this afternoon, and I liked them both. Margaret, who is to marry James of Scotland, is twelve. She's a merry girl, more like her brother Harry than the slender Arthur, but little Mary is quite different. She's only six, a very pretty child with curling fair hair, but very serious. "I will sing for you," she said. And she did, amazingly well, her little voice true and sweet. They say she will marry the Duke of Milan's son when she is old enough – unless, of course, they've found someone more important by that time.

I'm glad I was not born a royal child. It must be hard to grow up knowing you will be given to a husband you have never met and may not even like – and at such an early age, too. I heard yesterday that King Henry's mother was only twelve years old when he was born, and she was so injured in having him that she was never able to bear another child. The woman who told me shook her head, not so much in pity as in disapproval. "Spoiled," she said, as if a queen is only valued for the children she produces. How odd that they are laden with jewels and fine clothes and yet their function is no different from that of the cow in the farmyard!

If Catherine is aware of these things, she never mentions them. We talk about the coming wedding, of course, but only in terms of dresses and flowers and whether she will really wear her hair loose as the English insist. She is the centre of all attention and loves every moment of it, but people only flock round her because she is the Princess of Aragon. They do not know Catherine as a real person and I suspect that they don't want to. It's not their concern.

This afternoon there was a great argument about hoops. The Spanish style is to wear a hoop under one's skirt so it stands out from the body, but the English don't do this. They let the dress fall about one's natural form, and we are enchanted with the idea. Fancy being able to move freely instead of being encased in a framework that makes you look like a hand-bell! And what a chance to show off the charms of a slim figure! Doña Elvira, needless to say, is all disapproval. She thinks the English style is indecent, and goes around muttering about "hussies looking as if they're wearing their night clothes." In her case, concealment is kind, but I don't see why those of us with less bulk to hide should go on being so restricted. Admittedly, it would be an immense amount of work to reshape all those skirts to hang properly without a hoop underneath, and we couldn't do it before the wedding. But afterwards – now, that's a different thing.

13th November 1501

Uncle Rod seems to take little pleasure in all the excitement and festivity. He shook his head this afternoon when I spoke to him about it, and said Queen Isabella would not approve of such gaudy extravagance. In her last letter to him, she remarked that money would be better spent in taking care of Catherine's long-term welfare – but that is not the Tudor way. Uncle Rod says their main aim is to impress the foreign royal families, because – and he glanced round to make sure nobody was listening – compared with those old ruling dynasties, the Tudors are an upstart lot with only a very slender claim to being royal at all. King Henry's mother, Lady Margaret Beaufort, is of royal stock, but on his father's side he comes of unruly Welsh landowners with a taste for fighting and good living. The crown was put on his head in all the blood and confusion of a battle fought at Bosworth Field, and they say it was retrieved from a thorn bush, where it had rolled from the head of the dead Richard III. Since then, Henry has tried throughout his reign to keep the peace, and he has succeeded in this – but his real battle is to win the respect of Europe's ancient royal families and he goes about that with the energy and determination of a soldier.

14th November 1501

The wedding. And what a day it's been! A whirlwind of colour and pageantry and feasting and wine – heavens, how these English drink! They are said to be the most truculent, law-resistant people in Europe, united among themselves only when fighting a common enemy, but their appetite for revelry is almost frightening. The King had caused the fountains to flow with burgundy wine after the marriage was celebrated, and the crowds were gulping it from their cupped hands, yelling and cheering, surging to and fro, careless of those who had fallen insensible and were being trampled over.

Catherine remained serene throughout it all. She looked lovely – as fresh and young as a girl making her First Communion – in her gown of white satin and with her long hair held by a circlet of gold and pearls. Those of us who had sat for so long stitching pierced seed pearls on to her veil with fine gold thread were rewarded when we saw her standing in that shimmer of delicate brightness. I wish Mama could have seen it – she would have been so proud.

Arthur, too, looked beautiful in his white clothes, and in the cathedral the pair of them stood out like two white swans against the deep, rich scarlet of the draperies and the massed gorgeousness of the courtiers. Margaret was gowned in cloth of gold as befits the future Queen of Scotland, and little Mary wore a dress of crimson velvet. Harry was in a richly embroidered tunic and a fur-trimmed cloak, and when the ceremony ended, it was he who escorted Catherine down the aisle to the waiting people massed outside. His face was proud and unsmiling, and I had the feeling that he was impatient with his youth, cursing it for casting him as the second son and not the elder.

We came in grand procession to Baynard's Castle, and feasted throughout the afternoon and evening. Gold platters gleamed in the light of hundreds of candles, and servants came in with course after course of soups and pies and roast meats (venison, rabbit, goose, swan and suckling pig) and then great cheeses and sweets (jellies and trifles and brandy-soaked cakes) – all served with an abundance of wine.

And then – I still blush a little when I think of this – the time came for the last part of the ceremony. Arthur and Catherine were escorted upstairs in a rather drunken procession headed by the Earl of Oxford. There were several bishops as well, and boys swinging censers, and I don't know how many noblemen (most of them friends of Arthur's), laughing and making ribald jokes. Doña Elvira went as well, and so did I, together with Catherine's maid Maria and quite a lot of Spanish courtiers. I knew what was to happen. Doña Elvira had explained that it was a religious ceremony, and I watched while we all stood round the damask-curtained bed with the royal coat of arms embroidered at its head. The covers had been turned down to expose the undersheet and pillows, and amid the chanting of prayers, the Earl of Oxford laid himself down, first on Arthur's side of the bed then on Catherine's, and holy water was sprinkled on the bed. I thought it would make it dreadfully damp, but Doña Elvira was crossing herself fervently and so was everyone else, so I joined in. Arthur was being slapped on the back by his friends. His face looked very pale, and he took another long draught of wine, but one of the bishops frowned and removed the goblet from his hand, speaking to him in a stern whisper.

After that the crowd was shepherded out, though not without the shouting of some final bawdy jokes. I was not sure of their meaning – it's something men laugh about between themselves – but I felt terribly embarrassed for Catherine, who throughout all this had stood with clasped hands and lowered eyes. Doña Elvira kissed her and said she must be of good courage. Then she, too, went out. Maria and I stayed as Catherine had asked us, and we went into a small adjoining room to help her undress. Two men-servants were doing the same for Arthur.

Catherine was shivering although a fire burned in the bedroom. We slipped the fine lawn nightdress over her head (I had banded it with Italian reticella work at the neck and sleeves) and Maria offered her a silk shawl to put about her shoulders. Catherine shook her head. Her hands were clasped at her mouth, and I could not tell whether she was praying or blowing on her fingers. "You must go now," she said. I hugged her, and could feel her body trembling, but she would never admit to being afraid.

I am writing this in the small room which I share with Maria, who is asleep. I wonder what has happened to Catherine this night. We used to giggle so often about the things grown-ups did when they went to bed together, but neither of us could do more than guess what they got up to. We knew it resulted in the birth of a baby, but exactly how the baby was started remained a mystery to us. When I was twelve and one day found I was bleeding, my mother gave me cloths to use and said it showed I was now a woman – but I didn't want to be a woman, I wanted to go on playing under the olive trees and having no cares.

Tomorrow, the mystery will be explained, for Catherine will surely tell me.

15th November 1501

I have learned nothing. Arthur came from the bedchamber late this morning, baggy-eyed and looking as any boy will look who has drunk far too much wine on the night before, but he managed to grin for his back-slapping friends. "This night I have been in the midst of Spain," he said, and they all cheered.

I went in to Catherine, who was still in bed. She looked very tired. I sat down beside her and took her hand, and she shrugged in answer to my unspoken question. "He snores," she said. "But he kissed me a lot." And that was all she told me. It's very disappointing.

24th November 1501

Uncle Rod was right about the Tudor determination to lay on a good show. The tournaments and jousting have been glorious to watch and the sumptuous banqueting has gone on and on. Every evening has been filled with music and dancing, and with astonishing theatrical events. Ingenious moving platforms brought in pageant after pageant – great structures peopled with choristers and actors, with gold and silver wolves that were really men and, amazingly, a ship in full sail that moved as though floating on water. Such artistry! And when the displays were over, musicians played for dancing. Catherine and I performed a Spanish seguidilla and everyone clapped and cheered us, then young Prince Harry danced with his sister Margaret. He is a great expert for one so young, quick and neat – but he was soon too hot in the many layers of his embroidered clothes (beautiful the way the fine-worked shirt sleeves are allowed to show through the slashed doublet), so he simply stripped off his overgown and tossed it aside, never breaking the rhythm as he danced on.

The last celebration was the best. After a banquet in the Parliament Chamber, they brought on what looked like a giant lantern as big as a bedchamber, with light glowing from inside its translucent panels – and within it were twelve beautiful ladies. It was as if we looked into a private fairyland. After this there arrived a towering, fantastic chapel of many layers and compartments, with children singing at its upper windows while doors below opened to release a whole colony of baby rabbits that ran everywhere. Then eight ladies appeared at other doors in the intricately painted structure, and opened basketfuls of white doves that flew round the vast hall and settled on the high beams above us. Glorious, glorious.

But yesterday the festivities ended, and the Spanish nobles and their ladies who came only for the wedding are preparing to leave. Everything seems very flat.

26th November 1501

The King had one more trick up his sleeve. This morning he asked Catherine and her ladies to come to his library, and while he was showing us the books with their beautifully painted pictures and their tooled and gilded covers, a man suddenly came out from behind the shelves, holding a great casket. He opened it at the King's instruction, and we all gasped, for it was full of magnificent jewellery – diamonds, sapphires, rubies and emeralds set into necklaces, coronets, rings, brooches and bracelets, all with intricate gold and silver work. The King told Catherine to take what she wanted, and she dipped her hand into the sparkling mass, lifting out one beautiful thing after another and exclaiming with delight at each one.

When she had made her choices, King Henry turned to us and said we, too, might select a gift. Doña Elvira took a large brooch set with rubies and garnets, and Maria had a delicate necklace of pearls and filigree silver. And I have an opal ring. The stone seems to glow with fire and blue sky, and it is the most wonderful thing I have ever owned.

29th November 1501

A bustle of packing is going on, for the court is soon to move from Baynard's Castle to Windsor. Catherine and what remains of her Spanish entourage will not be going with them. We are to move to a manor owned by Prince Arthur in a place called Bewdley, in Worcestershire.

There has been much debate, Uncle Rod confided to me, about whether Catherine and Arthur are old enough to live yet as man and wife. I couldn't see why not – what is the point of being married if your lives are not shared? But he looked reserved, as he often does, and reminded me that Catherine's brother, Juan, had died in the early months of his marriage to the Princess of Portugal – a terrible tragedy for Isabella and Ferdinand to lose their only son. The doctors thought, he said, that his death might have been caused by over-exertion. I do not see why marriage should be considered an exertion. At worst, it seems likely to be merely tiresome.

10th December 1501

There is hardly room for us all in this house, a cold place although Arthur has had glass put in the windows. We will move again to Ludlow Castle, on the borders of Wales, they say.

I am hurrying to finish embroidering a kerchief for Catherine's birthday in six days' time. It is a design of two birds and a twining of vine leaves, done in our Spanish blackwork, a style much admired here by the English ladies.

The weather is turning very cold.

15th January 1502

Today, Margaret will be officially betrothed to James IV of Scotland, though we will not be there to see it. Everyone says we are not missing much – a betrothal is not the same as a full-blown wedding – but any diversion would be welcome. This castle is dank and forbidding, and the misted mountains of Wales loom in a constant shroud of rain.

The procedures of royal weddings are very strange. Tomorrow there will be a proxy marriage, which is not the real thing but an exchange of vows made by stand-ins. Uncle Rod stood in for Catherine at her proxy wedding years ago, and I can't imagine anyone who looks less like a bride. Or even, for that matter, like a groom. Poor Uncle Rod – his wife died when Gonsalvo was born, and he has never replaced her, or even seemed to want to.

The court ladies here eye Catherine constantly – looking, I suppose, for that swelling of the waistline which means a baby is on its way. She remains as slim as ever, and spends much of her time praying in the strange, circular chapel (where every sound echoes in such a ghostly way). Praying for what? For a child, perhaps. Every royal family prays earnestly and constantly for sons, so that a supply of future kings may never be in doubt.

Maria whispers to me that in Arthur and Catherine's case there is doubt. One of the English chambermaids told her there was no blood on the royal sheets after their wedding night, and it seems there should have been if, as the woman put it, "they was properly married". This, too, I do not understand. Maria suggests that we are just the same as dogs and cats and horses – but surely human beings must be different? But the more I think of it, the more I fear she may be right.

There are alarming rumours about the Scottish king. If we do indeed behave like dogs, then he is a very active one, running after every bitch in sight. He has several children already, it is said, by different women whom he has loved but not married, and yet by all accounts he is a civilized man, scholarly and thoughtful, fond of music and art and keenly interested in science. According to Don Pedro de Ayala, he possesses instruments for the pulling out of teeth, but if he is called on to do this he pays the patient for the pain he has caused. He sounds a strange man, but an interesting one.

Uncle Rod says James did not really want to marry Margaret because he was deeply devoted to a woman called Margaret Drummond and refused to give her up. The court advisers were at their wits' end – and then Mistress Drummond conveniently died. It was poison, they say. Her two sisters who shared that final meal with her died also. I was appalled when I heard this. I asked Uncle Rod who had done it, but he shook his head. There are some things it is better not to know, he said.

15th February 1502

How long will this winter go on? I am sick with longing for Spain, where the sun shines even in these short days, and at night there is a blaze of stars. Here there is nothing but clouds and greyness and mud and the smell of wet stone. The Spanish courtiers share my discontent, and the only man here with any sense of purpose is Don Alessandro Geraldini, who taught Catherine and me when we were children and is now the priest who hears our confession. He at least is busy, trying to reassure us that we are not forgotten by God in this gloomy place.

27th March 1502

Catherine is ill. It began with a shivering fit that worsened by the hour, and now she lies half-insensible, on fire with fever yet pouring with perspiration. People here call it the sweating sickness. Their main concern is for Arthur, from whom Catherine caught the illness. He seems gravely ill, and although the doctors have bled him, he gets no better.

Doña Elvira says we should keep to our own rooms for fear of contagion, but Catherine calls for me in her delirium and how could I refuse to go to her? I sponge her face and body with warm water and dry her with a soft towel, but there is little else I can do except sit beside her so that she knows I am there. God protect her.

3rd April 1502

Prince Arthur died yesterday. A rider has been sent to London, to tell the King. I cannot write much. The fever caught me in turn and I am very weak.

20th April 1502

Catherine is alive, though she is still not well. Arthur lies in his coffin in the round chapel, and the air is heavy with the smell of herbs used by the embalmer. They will take him from here in three days' time to be buried in Worcester Cathedral.

I still feel shaky and exhausted. My back aches and my fingers are sore from hours of sewing. Countless bales of black silk have had to be cut and stitched into mourning dress for all the people here. Seven courtiers have died of the sickness, and I do not know how many servants.

4th May 1502

They are back now from the long business of the funeral. We watched the procession leave the castle ten days ago in torrential rain. Two Spanish noblemen rode at its head to represent Catherine, for she is too weak and ill to leave the castle. The coffin on its bier was pulled by four horses that laboured and steamed in the deep mud, and the men who splashed alongside had a hard job to keep the black canopy above it in place, stumbling and slipping as they were.

It got worse along the way, they tell me. The horses had to be replaced by oxen, whose powerful bodies and split hooves get a better grip. How shameful, though, that the corpse of gentle Prince Arthur should be hauled through the mire by beasts of the field.

Don Alessandro was with them. The rain stopped, he says, when they got to Worcester, so at least they could approach the cathedral with fresh black horses and some semblance of dignity. The assembled bishops looked magnificent, he said. I wish I had been there to see them. The English embroidery done for the church is famous all over Europe – the opus Anglicanum, it is called. I saw something of it at Catherine's wedding, but the robes worn for a funeral would be different, rich and dark.

Even at this time of grief, the Tudor gift of theatricality did not desert them. The coffin was covered in cloth of gold, and each nobleman who came in added his own golden pall, so that the dead prince lay under a mound of gleaming softness. A man of arms rode a black horse down the aisle of the cathedral, bearing Arthur's armour and his battle-axe, its head to the floor, and the court officials who carried golden staffs of office broke them in two and cast the pieces into the grave.

Catherine is beginning to regain her strength, but she seems lost and confused. At sixteen, she is a widow. The courtiers still cling to a faint hope that she may be carrying Arthur's child, but Doña Elvira shakes her head firmly at any mention of it. Catherine herself says nothing.

17th June 1502

At last the weather is dry. It is so good to go out of doors without the hems of one's dress becoming fouled with mud and one's shoes sodden. Catherine has had a letter from her mother, who has only just heard of Prince Arthur's death. Queen Isabella wants Catherine to come home to Spain. She says Ludlow Castle is an unhealthy place, and her daughter must leave it at once. A flutter of hope ran through all the Spaniards here, for all of us long for the sun and for warm tiles under our feet instead of these stinking rushes – but Catherine will not go. Her mouth is set in the obstinate line I know so well, and nothing will move her. The English must keep their side of the bargain, she says. She came here out of duty to marry Prince Arthur, on the promise that she would receive one third of the income from Wales, Chester and Cornwall. "They will not shuffle me off so easily," she says. And means it.

24th June 1502

One battle, at least, has been won. We are to move to London next week.

25th July 1502

We are at Durham House in the Strand, a road which runs by the River Thames in London. It's a grand house, built for the bishops of Durham but used mostly by visiting ambassadors. There's a garden laid out in the Italian style, with low hedges of clipped yew and rosemary, and high walls on either side with peach and plum trees trained against them. Stairs lead down to the river, where one may step into a boat to be rowed up to Westminster – far pleasanter than being jolted over the cobbles in a carriage.

Inside, there's a great hall, as there has been in all the other mansion houses I've seen, with a gallery at one end where musicians can play. This is summer, so it's not so cold, but smoke drifts past the carved screen from the kitchen and its fires, all part of the same room.

I'd hoped London streets would be cleaner than the muddy lanes of Wales, but there seems to be little difference. The paving hardly exists, and to make things worse, great troupes of oxen go through with barrels of water on their backs, churning up the mud and adding to it with their droppings. In the heavy warmth of the English summer the stink is dreadful.

Uncle Rod was here yesterday on official business. He brought the new envoy from Spain, a tall man called Hernan, the Duke of Estrada. They went to a long meeting from which Doña Elvira emerged looking flushed and angry, and I was longing to know what had happened. I caught my uncle in the garden for a few moments, and he told me there is a huge argument going on about Catherine's dowry. King Ferdinand paid the first half of it – 100,000 crowns – at the time of the wedding, but he now refuses to pay the second half. His daughter no longer has a husband, he says, so the English cannot claim that their side of the bargain has been kept. What's more, he wants the first half returned.

King Henry is furious, of course. He was counting on the money from Spain, and if he doesn't get it, he will not give Catherine her promised income. Indeed, he has not done so up until now, which is why none of her Spanish attendants has yet been paid. I told Uncle Rod how discontented we all feel, and asked if he could persuade the King to release just a little of the money, but he pursed his lips and shook his head. It would be indelicate to speak of money just now, he said, when the King and Queen are still in mourning for their son. I suppose diplomats have to learn to be patient.

26th July 1502

A letter has come from my mother. She has written only once before, in answer to my letter, and then she was full of concern for my welfare, but this time she mentions larger things. King Louis of France has invaded Italy, and there is a danger that Spain will be surrounded by hostile French forces. The English must stand by us, Mama says. Can't Uncle Rod start negotiating for a new marriage between Catherine and the King's younger son, Harry?

She doesn't realize that young Harry is still only eleven years old. A boy is not of legal age to marry until he is fourteen, so there are three years to wait. I think Catherine wishes it were otherwise, for there is something about Harry's broad-shouldered stance and direct, ruthless stare that disturbs every female heart, young though he is.

1st August 1502

The Spanish retainers here are growing louder in their complaints. They had hoped that Estrada was going to persuade the King to release some money so they would be paid, but nothing has happened and we are all penniless, Catherine as well. Fewer candles burn in the big iron holders, and the cooks present us with thin soup and tough meat, and their faces are full of contempt. Uncle Rod warns me to be careful what I say, but he explained privately that the King's prime concern is not with Catherine or Spain, but to bring about the wedding between Margaret and King James of Scotland. He needs this strong link, because he is always afraid that the Scots, who have no great love for England, will side with France. Margaret and James would have been married by now had it not been for Arthur's death and the mourning that followed it, and Henry is full of plans for sending his daughter on the long journey to Edinburgh, with all the great train of soldiers, attendants and courtiers who must go with her. So we will have to wait.

2nd August 1502

Today Doña Elvira flounced into the sewing room and flopped down so heavily that she sent scraps of silk flying everywhere, and burst into tears. Maria and I patted and consoled her, asking what was the matter, and she blurted out indignantly that she had only tried to be helpful. At a meeting with the King and my uncle and various dignitaries, she had said there was no reason why Catherine should not marry Henry's younger son, because her marriage to Arthur had not been "a proper one".

She was so agitated that she found herself blurting out what nobody has ever told me. It seems we do indeed copulate in the same way as animals, but when this happens to a girl for the first time, it causes her to bleed a little. In Catherine and Arthur's case, this did not happen, Doña Elvira says. She would have known, and so would the servants who changed the bed linen.

Apparently this makes a legal difference to Catherine's status. If her marriage to Arthur was not "consummated", as they call it, then it has no standing in law. Catherine remains a virgin – and this, Doña Elvira says, is a good thing because there is a passage in the Bible which forbids a man to marry his brother's widow. If Catherine really was Arthur's proper wife, then she could not marry his brother. Spain and England need a second marriage, so why are they not glad to know it is perfectly possible? She burst into noisy tears all over again, deeply offended that she had been told to be quiet and that she could not know what she was talking about.

I ran across to Uncle Rod's lodgings in the Strand this evening – a poor place, but he, too, has not been paid for months – and asked him to explain. Doña Elvira had put her foot in it rather badly, it seems, though she didn't know the other side of it. If Catherine was indeed not Arthur's "proper wife", then she has no right to the title of Princess of Wales, and no claim to be supported by King Henry. She cannot call herself a royal widow, because she was never a royal wife. She is nothing.

What a nightmare! We are caught in the middle of a dispute between kings, and either way, Catherine is the loser. I wish she would abandon this hopeless struggle, and go home. But she won't.

10th August 1502

The King's wife, Queen Elizabeth, has given Catherine some money. It's not a lot, Catherine confided as we sat stitching by the open window this afternoon, but at least she can pay her servants something of what they are owed. She glanced round to make sure the door was shut, then leaned towards me and said, "Do you know how she got it? She pawned some of the gold plate! Just fancy!"

I'm sure the King does not know. He lives with penny-pinching meanness, counting each candle and refusing to have a fire in his room even though he suffers from asthma and coughs constantly. How many candles will he have to save to pay for sending his daughter in splendour to marry the Scottish king? But as my uncle points out, Henry's concerns about Scotland come first at the moment. "I will keep trying, my dear," he said. "After all, I am a Spaniard. All my sympathies are with Catherine. But I have to be careful." No wonder he looks so tired sometimes.

23rd August 1502

Thomas Fish was here today, bringing Catherine some linen cloth and a length of fine lawn for a pair of embroidered sleeves. He had just come from Windsor, where he takes cloth regularly for the Queen. He also took her some cherry jam made by his wife, for Queen

Elizabeth is pregnant again, and has a great longing for the sharp taste of cherries. She has a pet monkey, he says, and this morning it tore to shreds a notebook in which the King keeps his private accounts. His roars of rage made the whole palace tremble, Fish said, and the monkey leapt to Elizabeth for protection. It would be safe with her, for she is a kind woman. Everyone prays she will have a healthy son to replace the lost Arthur. According to Fish, she told her grieving husband, "We are both young enough."

11th February 1503

The Queen has given birth to a daughter. There is rejoicing, of course, but of a slightly muted kind. A son would have been so much better. The little girl is to be called Katherine, spelled the English way, and all the Spaniards here are pleased.

13th February 1503

Queen Elizabeth is ill with the child-bed fever. We all went to Mass to pray for her safe recovery, but the smell of incense reminded me of the heavy scent that hung about Ludlow after Arthur had died. I must put such thoughts away, for fear they may come true.

20th February 1503

Our prayers did not save her. Sweet Elizabeth, Queen of England, died today on her 37th birthday. We are plunged again into mourning, and the baby Katherine is sickly and unlikely to live. Rain falls like tears.

4th March 1503

All London is in mourning. The state funeral of the Queen took place today at Westminster Abbey, and the chief mourner was Lady Katherine Courtney, after whom the baby, now also dead, had been called. So much for our Spanish hopes that it had been Catherine who was thus honoured.

It was beautifully done, of course. All along Cheapside, groups of 37 white-clad young girls, one for each year of the Queen's life, stood holding lit tapers, their heads wreathed in leaves and white flowers. Green and white, the Tudor colours. Candles burned in every parish church and torches flared in the sunless London streets, lighting the Queen to her rest.

Only a few weeks ago, anticipating the end of the year's mourning for Arthur, the Queen gave her daughter Margaret a magnificent gown of crimson, trimmed with the black squirrel fur they call pampilyon. Poor Margaret. Once again her marriage is postponed, and now she must face the journey to Scotland, when it comes, without the support of her beloved mother. She is a happy girl, given the chance, and these months of wearing black have damped her gay spirits. She was so glad when half-mourning allowed her to put a pair of embroidered white sleeves to her black dress, and then bright ones of orange sarcenet, which she loved. There was such a fuss in September when the court removed from Baynard's Castle to Westminster and she found that the orange sleeves had been left behind. Richard Justice, the Queen's Page of the Robes, was sent back to fetch them in a hired boat, which he was pleased about because he got paid extra. But now Margaret is in deepest black again, and her marriage will not take place until the summer.

6th March 1503

I found Catherine sitting by the window this morning, staring out at the river in something close to despair. She told me King Henry is thinking of marrying her himself now that Elizabeth is dead. Trying to cheer her up, I said, "But at least that way you would be the Queen of England" – but we both knew how hollow the words were.

Catherine looked at me very straight. "That's the wrong way, Eva," she said. "I *will* be queen one day, but not through marrying Henry. He is 46 and I am seventeen. With his bad chest and his gout, he might die within a couple of years, and then where would I be? A dowager whom nobody wants. Even if I bore his child, it would not be heir to the throne, for that position is Harry's. So I must be Harry's wife, not his father's."

She is right, of course, but it seems an impossible hope. Three years to wait before the royal boy is old enough to marry, and even then, she may not be the one they choose.

26th March 1503

The King's mother, Lady Margaret Beaufort, has come to Windsor to take over the running of the royal household. She is immensely capable – I remember well those magnificent banquets at the time of Catherine's wedding, all of which were organized by her.

Catherine is looking happier. A letter from Queen Isabella has dealt very firmly with Henry's idea of marrying her daughter. A barbarous notion, she told him. She suggests he should consider the widowed Queen of Naples, who would be much more suitable. Henry, apparently, is sending an envoy out there to inspect her and report back.

5th June 1503

At last Margaret has started on her journey to Scotland for her wedding with James. Henry has gone with her and all her retinue to his mother's mansion in Collyweston, the first step on the way, and they will all stay there for some days, hunting and disporting themselves. Margaret looked happy at last. She rode a white palfrey whose saddlecloth was embroidered with red roses and the lion of Scotland, and a litter fringed in gold followed her so that she could rest and be carried if she tired of riding. The whole train looked magnificent with its banners flying and the baggage carts striped in white and green, and crowds lined the streets to cheer her. The journey will take a month and the wedding is set for 8th August.

Meanwhile, our living conditions get worse. The bread is dark, musty-tasting stuff, made from bad flour that has started to ferment, and I suspect that mice have got at it, too. My stocks of thread and fabric are almost all used up, and I hate to think of the shameful inactivity that will follow when they are gone. Stripped of any pride in my skilled work, I will be reduced to a mere pauper, living on the crumbs of charity. I have not started on a new design for several weeks, and use my remaining silks for the careful mending of our clothes. As to my function as an interpreter, it is never called for now, although Catherine's grasp of English is not good. No English courtier has any need to speak to her. We are utterly forgotten.

23rd June 1503

Great news! Uncle Rod's patient diplomacy has succeeded at last – or something has – for a treaty of intended marriage between Harry and Catherine has been signed. There was such a spontaneous lifting of spirits among us that we needed to celebrate, so off we went down the river to Hampton Court, where Henry is building a great palace. Some of the English nobles came with us, for now they notice again that we exist, and several of them brought their dogs and crossbows and falcons for an afternoon's hunting in the countryside. The hawks wore little hoods when they were not flying – as ours do in Spain – but the stitchery of jewels and silver wire on these hoods was exquisite, making the birds look like little emperors as they sat in their darkness.

How strange the English are. In some ways they seem brutish and crude, full of uncouth vulgarity, and yet one hears music sung and played everywhere, and their clothes and linens are a glory of fine, colourful work. They seem to take a lusty joy in beauty of all kinds, and for this one can forgive them much.

5th October 1503

The King has granted Catherine an allowance of 100 pounds a month. She says it will not go far towards keeping us all and paying off her debts (and she wants to retrieve some of the plate she was forced to pawn), but it is much better than nothing.

Nobody gives Uncle Rod any credit for his part in this, though I know it was his work that brought it about. Doña Elvira treats him with open contempt, even though he spoke to the King on her behalf when the Spanish retainers were particularly unruly and caused him to give her a cloth-of-gold cap as a sign of his trust in her authority.

I know what lies behind the courtiers' lack of generosity towards my uncle, though nobody will voice it aloud – at least, not to me. They all know Rodrigo De Puebla is – or was – Jewish, though he converted to Christianity, as did the whole family. We didn't have much choice. Eleven years ago, Queen Isabella exiled all Jews, because for her, the Christian crusade is everything. My last letter from Mama says the Queen has permitted an Inquisition to be set up, testing the true faith of anyone about whom there is a shadow of doubt. There are rumours, she says, that its officers do not shrink from the use of terrible tortures or even death. For the first time, I am almost glad to be away from my country. My uncle and I never speak of the blood tie that binds us to a persecuted people – it is safer not to. But I see in his face sometimes a great weariness, and understand it.

Catherine, alas, has no understanding of my uncle's slow, careful work. She is impatient by nature, and much preferred Don Pedro Ayala of the wink and the charming smile – but he has been recalled to Spain.

8th November 1503

Fog shrouds the garden and hangs heavy over the river. There is no joy in going out, and the house is full of bickering and whispers. The question of whether Catherine's marriage to Arthur was a proper one is still being wrangled over, and my uncle says they are waiting for the Pope to give a judgement.

On another matter, though, my uncle has had a great success. He has brought about an agreement that English merchants trading in Spain will have all the rights and privileges of Spaniards, paying no extra charges and being free to load their cargoes without taxation. The same is true for Spaniards trading in England. I, at least, am very proud of him.

27th November 1503

The court has shifted its quarters from Windsor to Richmond. They move several times a year, lucky things, leaving the previous palace to be cleaned of soot and stripped of its vilely muddy and stinking rushes. I must say, much of the filth and stink in the houses is the fault of their occupants. If the men would refrain from pissing in the fireplaces, it would help. We Spaniards are not included in the "progress", as they call it, of the King and his court from one place to another, and Durham House is becoming disgusting.

18th February 1504

A young English lord wants to marry Maria de Rochas. He is the grandson of the Earl of Derby, very handsome in the fair, English way, and Maria is much in love with him. She went to Catherine to ask her blessing on the match, and to raise the question of a dowry. As one of Catherine's ladies, she should have dowry money provided by the royal purse – but Catherine has no funds to meet a request of this size. She has written to her father about it, but there is silence.

1st March 1504

Still no response from King Ferdinand on the question of Maria's dowry. She is beginning to fear that her suitor will look elsewhere.

9th March 1504

Poor Maria. Young Derby has withdrawn his offer, and she is utterly cast down. To make matters worse, Doña Elvira went to her and said she was glad the "silly affair" was over, for she wants Maria for her own son, Iñigo Manrique, master of the king's pages.

Catherine is furious. She suspects that Doña Elvira intercepted her letters to Ferdinand and made sure they were never sent. There was a tremendous quarrel this morning, and Catherine has told my uncle he must do something about replacing Doña Elvira. Uncle Rod looked helpless and pointed out that Queen Isabella has every faith in the duenna, who is charged to act as mother-substitute to Catherine while she is in England. Catherine retorted that she has no need of a mother-substitute. At eighteen, she is old enough to run her own affairs, and if she wants to get rid of Doña Elvira she should be able to do so. Doña Elvira remarked to her husband – but loud enough to be overheard – that it would take more than a jumped-up little Jewish go-between to remove her from her post. There are times when I hate her.

12th December 1504

Terrible news. We have just heard that Queen Isabella died two weeks ago, on November 26th. Catherine is huddled in her bed, weeping, and the courtiers stand in hushed groups, talking in low voices about what is to happen now. My uncle has gone to Windsor, to consult with the King.

If only Catherine's brother were still alive. So many problems would be solved were he here to step into his mother's shoes. Ferdinand has no claim in his own right, though as Isabella's widower he will fight hard to retain his kingship. Officially, the throne must go to Juana, Catherine's oldest sister – but she is married to Prince Philip of the Netherlands, and lives with him and their children in that flat, damp country which, people tell me, is even duller than England. It's a long way from Spain, and Dutch Philip will seem a strange king on the Spanish throne.

I wonder what Juana is like now. It's years since I have seen her. She was always very beautiful, as dark-eyed and graceful as a deer, and as easily startled. She fell deeply in love with Philip at first sight. Catherine used to read out her letters in those early days, and we would giggle over the passion they expressed. We were only young, and I suppose we found it a bit embarrassing. Does Juana still feel the same about him, I wonder? It is rumoured that Philip is constantly unfaithful to her. One of the English ladies smiled and said, "You know they call her Juana the Mad?" I hope it is not true.

16th December 1504

A letter came from Mama today. She speaks of the Queen's death, naturally. And she says Juana's nerves have been badly affected by her husband's infidelities – or so the gossip goes in Spain. Poor Juana. Has her husband really driven her mad?

Uncle Rod shrugged wearily when I spoke to him about it. Neither Philip nor Ferdinand want Juana to be thought sane, he says, because she in fact is the one who inherits the throne, and the big quarrel is between her father and her husband, both of whom want to rule in her place.

I so much hope for Catherine's sake that Ferdinand will manage to go on being king. It has been a terrible blow to her to lose her mother, and if her father is pushed out by Philip, it will be the end of all Catherine's hopes of a match with Harry. Her only value is in being the daughter of the Spanish king, and if that is lost, then so is everything else. But Philip is very powerful. His father, Maximilian, is Emperor of all the German states and of Austria, Flanders and Burgundy, a man of ruthless ambition, backed by all the authority of his aristocratic Habsburg family. I fear the worst, though I will not say so to Catherine.

Sometimes I wish I had someone else to talk to. Not just Uncle Rod, wise and kind though he is, but a friend my own age who would share my worries. Someone strong and dependable, a man-friend, I suppose I mean. Things are hard here, and getting harder. Catherine insists on using most of her allowance to reclaim her valuables, saying they are her only security for the future, but this means we are still half-destitute. We live on little but bread now, and on gristly bits of meat that we would have thrown to the dogs when we first came here. I can't afford to get my shoes mended, so my feet are constantly cold, and water-sodden if I try to venture out. But I must not complain to Catherine. Most of the Spaniards here are angry with her, and she has enough to bear.

7th May 1505

King Ferdinand has taken a new wife. She is Germaine of Foix – a French woman. The court is buzzing with indignation. One or two of the more thoughtful ones say it could be a clever move, designed to placate the French king and prevent him from attacking Spain, but most people simply think he is siding with Spain's enemy. That's what King Henry thinks, quite obviously. Thomas Fish was here again today, having come from Richmond with new supplies of linens and thread (thank God!), and he said Henry was raging, calling Ferdinand a turncoat and a traitor.

Catherine, too, is angry, but not with her father,

whom she trusts absolutely. She is sure that the marriage with Germaine is a means to win a breathing space from the French threat, and she berates our Spanish courtiers for not believing this. I don't know where she gets her energy and determination from. I do my best to feel as she does, but the effort leaves me tired and filled with secret doubts.

19th May 1505

Roger Fellowes has been paying me a lot of attention, and Catherine says he is in love with me. I do hope not. He has ginger hair and very pale eyelashes, and he blushes whenever he sees me. He comes of a good family and is very polite, but his is not the shoulder I would ever bury my face on. I cannot take seriously a man who looks like a peeled shrimp.

Our fears were well founded. Prince Harry has backed out of the marriage agreement, though rumour has it that he looks guilty and wretched, and he was talked into it by the King and his close adviser, a man called Thomas Wolsey. The excuse is that Harry was under legal age when he made the agreement, so it is not binding, but it's quite obvious that his father has decided to seek a better match for his son and heir than Catherine.

Harry will be fourteen tomorrow. In law he will be a man; and he looks a man, taller than most even now, and broad and strong. I had let myself dream that Catherine would marry him on this day, but all those hopes are ruined now. Harry himself has probably had no say in it. For the last year or more, his father has kept him tightly secluded, shut in a small room beyond the King's own chamber, and all the reports we have of the boy say he looks sulky and resentful, far from his old gaiety.

Catherine has said nothing about the new announcement. Her face is pale, but her mouth is firmly set and her fierce look deters anyone from mentioning it. This evening, as we struggled to find something edible on a couple of herrings that had been far too long out of the sea, she said to me quietly, "Harry and I *will* be married, Eva. But first the old king will have to die." I suppose the words shocked me, for she smiled as she broke off a piece of bread and glanced round to make sure nobody else had heard. "Time is on my side," she said. "You'll see."

20th September 1505

The Spanish have abandoned the trade treaty my uncle brought about, and the effect is disastrous. Eight hundred merchants have just come back from Spain, complaining that they have been ruined by the extortionate prices asked by the Spaniards, and demanding that Henry do something about it. So Henry shouted at Uncle Rod, blaming him for the treaty's collapse. He could be heard all through the court, it is said, bellowing that De Puebla had betrayed him. So unfair.

22nd September 1505

In his fury with all things Spanish, the King has withdrawn Catherine's allowance, and she is in despair. How is she to run this house and feed all these people, no matter how meanly, on no money whatsoever? Durham House is a wretched place now, the linen soiled and torn and the stink of half-rotten fish and meat mingling with the general reek of sodden rushes and filth.

Doña Elvira goes round saying that King Ferdinand obviously knows nothing of our plight, otherwise he would do something about it. She blames poor Uncle Rod, whom she calls "that little rat" for having kept Ferdinand in the dark. My uncle protests that he is in constant contact with the Spanish king and has repeatedly told him of the situation, but Doña Elvira sweeps past him with her nose in the air. She is constantly cooing over Catherine and reminding her of how badly we are all treated, but she bullies everyone else. Poor Maria de Rochas has had to agree to marry Doña Elvira's stuck-up son, because her English admirer stopped admiring her when she became as poor and shabby as the rest of us.

23rd September 1505

Doña Elvira has suggested that Catherine should meet with her sister, Juana. The region of Calais in France still belongs to England, and they could meet there, she says, a convenient halfway point between London and the Netherlands. Once Juana understands how miserable her sister is, she will tell their father, and something will be done about it.

Catherine is very excited by the idea. I can see why – she is lonely here, and it's a long time since she saw her sister. And, to my sadness, she believes Doña Elvira's story that my uncle is not telling Ferdinand of her plight.

Doña Elvira says the meeting will be simple. Her brother, Don Juan Manuel, is the Spanish ambassador at the court of Emperor Maximilian, so he knows Philip well and will organize everything. The pair of them plan that King Henry himself will go with Catherine, and Philip will escort Juana – it will be a splendid meeting. Catherine agrees, and she has written a letter to Philip, putting the suggestion to him. And I told Uncle Rod.

29th September 1505

A reply from Philip has come back very quickly, and Catherine seems delighted.

30th September 1505

Heavens, what drama! My uncle was here this morning and, as we stood talking, Catherine came up with Philip's letter, as well as one she had just written to Henry, asking him if he will go with her to the meeting. Uncle Rod looked appalled, but he is always diplomatic. He suggested politely that Catherine should hand over both letters to him and let him do the negotiations – but Catherine would have none of that. Her chin was in the air in that obstinate way I know so well, and she told my uncle she was quite capable of managing her own affairs, and if he had anything to say about it, he had better speak to Doña Elvira. So off she went with the letters, leaving Uncle Rod to brave the dragon.

I caught him later, and he said Doña Elvira had promised to make sure the letter to the King was not sent. "Don't you see?" he said. "It will cause the final rift with Ferdinand if Henry goes off to a private meeting with Philip – a diplomatic disaster." He didn't trust Doña Elvira, feeling pretty sure she would send the letter all the same. He went back to his lodgings because his landlady would have his supper ready, but he left his servant at Durham House, to watch what happened.

After that, the fun really started. The servant saw Doña Elvira give the letter to a man who rode off into the night, and rushed across to tell Uncle Rod, who came hobbling as fast as his gouty legs would carry him to tackle Catherine about it. I've never seen him so upset – he was actually in tears – but then, of course, he was looking at the ruin of all his careful work to keep good relations between England and Spain.

For once, Catherine listened. I watched her face darken as she heard how Doña Elvira had for years been sending court secrets to her brother, where they were fed straight to Philip and Maximilian. For all the flattering talk about King Ferdinand, she had in fact been working against him. She and her brother wanted to see Philip on the throne of Spain, and the proposed meeting of royal sisters was simply a way to bring Henry into personal contact with Philip, perhaps leading to a pact between them to launch a joint attack on Ferdinand. No wonder Uncle Rod was so upset!

It was too late to stop Catherine's letter from reaching the King, but my uncle explained to her that if the meeting went ahead, it might result in her father's exile or even his death.

He didn't have to explain any further. Catherine sat down at her desk and dipped a pen into the inkwell. "Tell me what I must write," she said. And at Uncle Rod's dictation, she put down an apology for not having understood the situation, and begged the King's pardon for having suggested a meeting which he might have found embarrassing. Then she went to see Doña Elvira.

We all know Catherine has a temper, but I have never heard such an outburst of fury as the one which followed. She berated the duenna at a pitch that could be heard all over the house, and we listened in guilty delight to the goings-on. Whenever Doña Elvira tried to say anything, the torrent of words got faster and louder, until the dusty tapestries on the walls seemed to quiver with Catherine's rage. When Doña Elvira at last came out, her face was crimson and her mouth set like a trap. She met nobody's eye but went to her bedroom and slammed the door.

23rd October 1505

Doña Elvira left this morning, saying she needs to consult a doctor in the Netherlands about her eyes, though we have never heard her complain of poor sight. She has taken her husband, her son and the unfortunate Maria, and nobody expects to see them back.

6th November 1505

Everything is changing. After Doña Elvira left, Catherine went to King Henry and said she was now alone in running Durham House and she really must have some money.

It was a mistake. When Henry heard of the duenna's departure, he said Catherine could not possibly remain unchaperoned and in charge of such a big household. Fifty Spanish retainers was an unreasonable number anyway. Most of them could be sent home and Catherine could move into court with a small staff.

There was a huge argument about who should go back to Spain and who should stay, followed by a commotion of packing, and tomorrow those of us who remain will go to Richmond Palace for the winter. Somehow, I regret leaving Durham House, squalid though it has become. It has been our own place, and now we will have no proper home, only what rooms the English choose to give us in their various grand houses. Catherine does not complain – she says the move may be useful. I know what she means – she will be nearer to Prince Harry and to the centre of whatever is going on. But I am leaving Uncle Rod behind in his shabby lodgings, and I feel bereft.

13th January 1506

Great excitement has seized the court. Philip of the Netherlands and Juana, with an enormous entourage in a great fleet of ships, were caught in a storm while sailing to Spain to claim the throne from Ferdinand, and they have been blown ashore in England. They are at a place called Melcombe Regis in Dorset, amid the wreckage of their fleet. Several ships were sunk and the surviving ones are battered and broken. Philip sent a rider to London, to tell Henry of his plight, so a train of baggage-waggons and horses and carriages has been despatched for their rescue, and here we are in a ferment of preparation to receive the royal guests.

How ironic that the meeting which Doña Elvira failed to bring about has been achieved after all, by foul weather! My uncle is in constant consultation with the King, planning what advantage can be seized from this opportunity. Weather, he explained to me, is neutral. There is nothing clandestine about this meeting – it is pure chance, and nobody can accuse Henry of plotting. But the situation in Spain remains very delicate, with Ferdinand moving ever closer to an understanding with France. He has signed a treaty with Louis XII which, among other things, prevents Philip and Juana from setting foot on French soil, which is why they had to make their journey to Spain by sea. It may be, Uncle Rod says sadly, that Henry will have to seek Philip's friendship now rather than Ferdinand's – but he still hopes to prevent an all-out attack on Catherine's father.

Catherine herself is suddenly the centre of attention again. Since moving into Richmond we have been treated like poor relations, housed in mean little rooms and openly despised, but now, as Juana's sister, Catherine must be made presentable. We have been given some silk to make her a new gown, and a frenzy of cutting and stitching is going on.

29th January 1506

A second herald arrived from Philip this morning, to say the procession from Dorset is near London now, and should arrive tomorrow. To Catherine's disappointment, Juana is not with them – the near-shipwreck and the drowning of so many people has upset her so greatly that she is unfit to travel.

31st January 1506

They are here! There seemed no end to the pouring in of horses and carriages, nobles, attendants and soldiers – huge numbers of soldiers. Evidently Philip has every intention of routing Ferdinand by force if necessary. Lady Margaret, the King's mother, has made her preparations wonderfully well, and has coped with the great invasion smoothly. She has sent the soldiers off to Croydon, where they will be housed in the Archbishop of Canterbury's palace in far more comfort than they are used to.

Philip himself was ushered into the royal rooms that are hung with tapestries and cloth of gold, and he could not help being impressed when he saw the chamber where he is to sleep. He guessed correctly that it must be Henry's own room, the walls swathed in crimson velvet caught between embroidered bosses depicting the royal coat of arms, but Henry gave a casual shrug and said it was merely a guest room. Nobody smiled, though we all knew how much frantic stitching and decorating has gone on. The King has moved into the rather bleak emptiness of Queen Elizabeth's rooms, closed and unused since her death.

Now we are set for days of jousting and tournament and nights of revelry. Harry's little sister, Mary, is ten years old now, very grave and self-possessed, and she enchanted them all with her skilled playing of the lute. Catherine has taught her a lot, for she herself is a good lutenist. And Catherine is in her element, laughing and beautiful, gently flirting with the Lowland nobles while always retaining a royal dignity. We performed several Spanish dances this evening, and then she partnered Harry in a dance. The pair of them move with a grace and neatness that makes them seem one thing. Little has been seen of Henry or Philip, who have been closeted together almost incessantly. They seem to have taken a great liking to each other – and of course they have one important thing in common. They both hate the idea of losing power to Ferdinand.

9th February 1506

Henry announced today that a treaty of close friendship with Philip has been signed. A whole string of royal marriages has been proposed as well. Mary is promised to Philip's young son, Charles, and Henry himself may possibly marry Philip's sister, Margaret of Savoy, though the lady has not been consulted about it. And Harry, it is suggested, could take as his bride Philip's daughter, Eleanor. I saw the shadow that crossed Catherine's face when she heard this. She is still utterly convinced that Harry is hers, but I cannot see how they can consider her a possibility now that her father has become the common enemy of Philip and Henry.

Harry was not present to hear these proposals. He has been sent at the head of a big retinue to fetch Juana from the West Country. Bets are being laid as to whether he will succeed, but I am sure he will. Nobody could refuse Harry when confronted by the full force of his charm and determination.

10th February 1506

He succeeded! Juana is here, white-faced and huge-eyed, a little inclined towards tears – but surely not mad? She greeted King Henry with tremulous dignity, and as he gave her his arm to escort her in, I saw him look down at her with a curiously tender concern. Philip, on the other hand, greeted his wife with no more than conventional courtesy, and I saw her lips quiver as he walked away, though she managed to retain her composure.

Henry announced this evening that Philip has agreed to hand over the fugitive Earl of Suffolk, who has been living in the Netherlands for many years.

The two royal men are on fire with their friendship and the power of the promises they have made to assist each other against all enemies, and Uncle Rod has sent a desperate message to Ferdinand of Aragon, warning him of the forces allied against him.

Tomorrow Catherine and her remaining retainers are to be sent back to Richmond, so she has had little chance to talk to her sister. And I have a new reason to regret leaving here. Tonight, I met a man who enchants me. He was sitting by the lily pool where great goldfish swim slowly under the round leaves. I had gone out to cool my flushed face, heated from dancing, and did not see him until he said, "It's better out here. Sane."

He came with Philip's entourage. He is their court jester, and they call him "Mr John" – perhaps that's as close as they can get to his real name, Michel Valjean. Or perhaps he took it as a stage name. I find myself remembering every word of the conversation I had with him. Such a down-to-earth conversation, about the absurdities of royalty and the dangers and pleasures of trying to cheer them up. "Your King Henry is hardly a laugh a minute, is he?" he said. "Hard work getting him to crack a smile. But he gave me ten pounds for amusing him, so I must have done something right."

He took my hand when we turned to come in, and ran his thumb over my knuckles. "A nice hand," he said. "Practical."

But tomorrow I have to go back to Richmond.

1st April 1506

All Fools' Day. So I think of my Fool, of course. My Michel. Foolishly, I expect. He has moved on now, to other courts, other fishponds, warm and still in the heat of Spain.

28th June 1506

Prince Harry's fifteenth birthday.

For us, there is no cause for celebration. Again, we shift in our ragged clothes from one contemptible place to another. When we came back to Richmond, we were put in rooms above the stable, dusty and mouse-infested, and now we are in a filthy, run-down manor in Fulham.

Nobody grumbles any more, we are past that. Everyone is aware of Catherine's simmering rage, but the determination in her set face commands respect. There are no carping remarks now about her pawning off the remaining plate and jewels, though we all know the goldsmiths charge her high interest rates, fearing they will never see their money again. Occasionally Henry gives her a hundred pounds or so, but it is swallowed up at once in reclaiming some of the pawned treasure. She cannot be stripped of everything, she says, if she is to have some self-respect when she marries Harry. I can't understand how she goes on believing this will happen.

18th October 1506

An extraordinary blow has fallen. We heard today that Philip of the Netherlands is dead. Philip the Handsome, as they all called him. Philip the Faithless, breaker of Juana's heart. Philip the friend of Henry and newly arrived king of Castile.

What will happen now? I suppose this means Ferdinand will resume his throne, ruling on behalf of Juana, whom he has always declared to be insane.

I am kept busy mending Catherine's gowns. I darn the tears and thin patches, then decorate them with flat-stitch embroidery, but nobody is taken in. We are destitute.

19th October 1506

I walked to the Strand late this afternoon, to see my uncle. He begins to look very old and worn. He says that now Philip is dead, Henry will have to win the favours of Emperor Maximilian, Philip's father. No lucky storm will blow him into Henry's court, so other means must be found. Henry is going to lend him 100,000 gold crowns.

23rd October 1506

A letter came from Mama today. She tells a terrible story about Juana. She would not leave Philip's body, sitting beside it in the chapel day and night, not seeming to hear what anyone said to her. When at last she fell asleep, they took it out of her sight, but she woke in a frenzy and summoned her servants, and when she found the coffin she bade her men take it on their shoulders and follow her, and she set out across the hills in a strange, wild procession with her dead husband. Heaven knows what has happened now – Mama does not say.

1st March 1507

Harry's elder sister, Margaret, gave birth to a son ten days ago. He is the first of a new generation of Tudors – that is, if they will think of him as a Tudor up there in Scotland. The boy is to be called James, after his father. I can hardly meet Catherine's eye, knowing what everyone is saying. If only she had managed to give Arthur a son, we would have had a royal boy here in London. As it is, this newborn half-Scot stands next to Harry and even, at some time in the future, above him, for this new James could inherit the crowns of both England and Scotland.

13th July 1507

Catherine is triumphant. After all these years, her father has sent her 2,000 ducats, apparently justifying all her faith in him. Now that Philip is dead, Ferdinand is again secure as the ruler of Spain, and he needs to patch up his damaged friendship with England. Perhaps I am cynical, but I suspect that his sudden generosity is more to please Henry than his daughter – but I will not say so, of course.

Catherine sat down at once to write a long letter of thanks to her father, and as she sealed it, she told me she had asked him to send a different ambassador. She made no explanation, just said we needed someone new. Did I not love her like a sister, I would feel deeply hurt.

2nd August 1507

I see now what Catherine was after. A fat package arrived from Spain this morning, and it contained the official papers which make Catherine herself Ferdinand's ambassador. Uncle Rod was at the court, and when he heard this he put his fingers to his forehead and closed his eyes in despair.

I, too, find it hard to believe Catherine can be a diplomat. She is clever, certainly, and tenacious, but her iron determination to marry young Prince Harry and be the Queen of England colours all her thinking, and I doubt whether she has it in her to learn the subtle arts of statesmanship. But I may be wrong. She learns fast.

3rd September 1507

Michel is here! A servant said this morning, with the curl of the lip I am used to, "There is a person in the kitchen wishing to see you."

And there he was, thinner than ever after long weeks of travel on foot. There was no place for him in the Spanish court once Philip had died, and he is going to make his way to the Netherlands, where Philip's eight-year-old son Charles is being cared for until such time as he is old enough to marry Mary.

If Michel secretly hoped he would be taken on as court jester here, he is out of luck, alas. Henry's generosity on the previous occasion was, I'm afraid, more to impress Philip with his careless munificence than to reward Michel's talent, and there are already a number of fools and entertainers here, some of them "innocents" whose drooling antics never make me smile.

Michel is not a welcome guest. He sleeps in the hay-loft and, did I not take him bread and meat scrounged from the kitchen, he would have nothing.

We walk together in the evenings and kiss, and I wish with all my heart that I could be with him always – but we can make no plans. Michel says he has no belief in plans, anyway. "Any wise man should lock them in a box and throw away the key," he says. "Half the world consists of key-seekers, you see, and what would they do if keys were not thrown away for them to seek?" I love him so much.

9th October 1507

The King is interested in marrying Juana. Catherine is all in favour of it. She has started to think diplomatically now and actually consults Uncle Rod quite often, with a new respect for his opinions. She can see that the alliance Henry hopes to forge with Philip's father, Maximilian (a brigand of a man, if you ask me), spells out a terrible danger to her father, so any link between England and Spain is to be welcomed.

Henry is concerned about the question of Juana's sanity, of course, having heard the tale of the mad coffin-carrying. My uncle assures him that Juana was simply driven beyond endurance by her beloved husband's flagrant infidelity to her. It is true that she did once attack one of his mistresses with a pair of scissors but, given steady kindness and care, she would very probably recover her stability. Henry was much taken with her during her short visit, and likes to regard her as an ill-used woman who is waiting for him to rescue her. The Tudors are incurably romantic.

24th December 1507

Henry's loan to Maximilian has had the desired effect. Last week the pair of them signed a treaty which pledges them to be allies, and in celebration we are all to have a merry Christmas, officially sanctioned. Free hogsheads of wine have been distributed throughout London, and singing and roistering is well under way. Bonfires burn in the streets and the church bells ring.

Needless to say, Catherine does not rejoice. She looks narrow-eyed and grim, but I cannot share her concerns at the moment. Today I had a letter from Michel, to read again and again, knowing his hand touched the paper and formed the words. I am as happy as any of the people in the streets, and wish I could join them in their singing and dancing.

14th January 1508

Catherine is demanding again that her father must send a new ambassador, but for a different reason this time. We must have a man of good standing, she says. Both she and my uncle (who has not been paid for many years) are too shabby and poor to be treated with any respect at court. It is time Spain was represented by a man of some grandeur.

16th February 1508

Ferdinand evidently saw the sense of Catherine's request. A new ambassador arrived today. His name is Gutierre Gomez de Fuensalida, and he is indeed grand – positively arrogant, in fact. He wears his fine clothes with the panache of a matador, and seems to regard Henry as the bull of England – a country which, he says, only understands a rough hand. Catherine enjoys his flamboyant company, but Uncle Rod is appalled. He is in bed with gout, but he sent his son Gonsalvo to warn Fuensalida to tread carefully, as relations between England and Spain are in a very delicate state.

Fuensalida took no notice but marched straight in to see the King, who has been ill with a chest complaint this winter. No wonder he felt so sure of himself – he had brought with him Catherine's long-unpaid dowry, 65,000 ducats of Aragon!

Suddenly, Catherine is back in favour. Fuensalida reported that Henry, though weak and forbidden to talk for long, spoke of her with great warmth and said there was nobody he would rather see as wife to his son.

"Didn't I tell you!" Catherine said to me this evening, sketching a dance across the floor in her delight. "Now we'll see!" But I feel uneasy about the new ambassador. Already people are finding him rude and objectionable, and I fear we are in for trouble.

19th February 1508

Trouble, indeed. It turns out that the 65,000 ducats does not represent the whole of Catherine's dowry. The rest is to be paid in jewellery and plate. Henry's officers asked whether the ambassador had brought these articles with him, and he pointed out that Catherine had been supplied with them in 1501, when she had married Arthur. But those had become Arthur's property when he had taken Catherine as his wife, the officers pointed out. Was Ferdinand now trying to pay his daughter's dowry with goods already in English possession? And why had he kept Catherine so deprived of her rightful dowry that she was forced to pawn these goods?

Fuensalida promptly pointed out that it was Henry's miserliness that had driven her to do this, and the meeting turned into a shouting match.

4th March 1508

Henry is recovered enough now to deal with Fuensalida himself, but every time they meet, it ends in a quarrel. My uncle, also a little better though still hobbling, does what he can to soothe the King's feelings and moderate Fuensalida's behaviour, so of course he is accused afresh of being on Henry's side. A dreadful situation.

27th March 1508

There is sad news from Scotland. Margaret has lost her baby son, little James. He died just a month ago, on February 27th, six days after his first birthday. She expects a second child this summer, but my heart goes out to her, especially as she stands in the middle of a worsening disagreement between England and Scotland. To have an English royal father and a Scottish royal husband puts her in a terrible position.

Last week Henry arrested the Earl of Arran for travelling across England without the necessary papers when he was on his way home to Edinburgh from France. The papers were just a technicality that Henry could have overlooked – but he knew the Earl had been conferring with Louis XII in Paris, and felt sure the French and the Scots were ganging up against England.

Unfortunately, the Earl is a cousin of King James, and a close personal friend, so there is great Scottish fury at his arrest. Catherine thinks Henry was perfectly justified. Although she likes Margaret, and is sorry for her, she has no patience with the Scots. As far as she can see, their old friendship with France makes them the enemies of Spain and of England. She reminds me so much of her dead mother these days. Queen Isabella, too, saw things in black and white. Those who were not with her were against her, with no word to be said in their favour. Thomas Wolsey has been sent to Edinburgh to try to smooth things over. I hope he succeeds.

21st June 1508

I cannot believe what has happened. Poor Uncle Rod – the whole thing is appalling. He was at a long, difficult meeting this afternoon with the King and the new ambassador, Fuensalida, about the situation between Scotland and France. Things are a little better since Wolsey's intervention, and Uncle Rod managed to persuade the King to be slightly more friendly to Catherine's father in Spain – but when they emerged from the chamber, Fuensalida turned on my uncle, shouting that his "pussyfoot tactics" were useless. Why did he not *demand* that Henry treat Ferdinand with more respect?

For once in his life, my uncle lost his temper. "I can do no more!" he shouted back. "I cannot twist the ears of the King of England!" And at that point, Fuensalida produced a letter from King Ferdinand and gave it to him. It was a letter dismissing Dr Rodrigo De Puebla from his post. He then said, with a triumphant smile on his face, that he had been carrying two letters from the Spanish king ever since his arrival here, one praising De Puebla for his excellent work, and the other dismissing him. Fuensalida had been waiting to choose which one to deploy. And he had now chosen.

I am so angry. This arrogant, tactless, trouble-making man has undone all Uncle Rod's years of faithful work, and he has proved, too, that Ferdinand never really trusted my uncle or liked him. I didn't know at first what had happened, but when I saw my uncle leaving the palace, he looked old and shrunken, and leaned heavily on the arm of his servant. I was so troubled that I ran up to ask if he was all right, and he shook his head. I went with him to his lodgings and stayed there for the night, sleeping on the couch in his room. He seems utterly collapsed.

22nd June 1508

Uncle Rod is still in his bed. He says he will never get up again. This morning he wrote a letter to King Ferdinand, then sealed it and gave it to me. "Make sure it is sent, my dear," he said. "There is no one else I can trust." Then he said it would be his last letter. "I will not have to trouble you again." I wept as I took it from his hand, but he seems beyond tears.

15th July 1508

The court has moved to Windsor where we are wretchedly quartered in rooms above the stables. I hate to be so far from Uncle Rod.

2nd August 1508

We have just heard that Margaret had a little girl two weeks ago, but the child did not live, and Margaret is ill. How ironic it is that King James has so many healthy children by his various mistresses, but his legal wife struggles to produce a living baby.

Henry has released the Earl of Arran from prison, and James has promised that he will not send an army to France, to fight on the side of the French king. Catherine gave a cynical smile when she heard this. "An easy promise," she said. "So he keeps his army in Scotland – but who is to say he will not attack us from across our northern border? He has made no promise about that."

20th September 1508

The whole court fled to the country three weeks ago, in panic because of an outbreak of plague in London. They took every available horse and carriage and all the supplies they needed, but not one of them suggested that Catherine should go with them. We were left here in Windsor, in our squalid rooms over the empty stables, and we foraged in the garden and the fields for food. It was humiliating that the peasants, who are so poor, gave us milk and cheese. Catherine assured me she would pay them, but I don't know how. Maybe she still has a few valuables that she can pawn, but if so, she keeps them hidden. However, we did not die or even become sick, and the courtiers are back now, chattering and gossiping like a flock of starlings.

They are all hysterically convinced that Henry means to attack Spain, and Fuensalida has actually written to Ferdinand, asking him to send a ship so that Catherine and her remaining household can be taken back to Granada before war breaks out.

Catherine is furious with him. He had no right to send such a letter without consulting her, she says. She has not struggled through all these years to cave in now, and whatever happens, she is staying here.

28th September 1508

I begged a lift to the Strand with a court lady who was going to visit her sister in London, and spent a day with Uncle Rod. He is still in bed, looking frail. I told him, truthfully, that Catherine now detests Fuensalida, and wishes she had listened more carefully to Uncle Rod's advice, and he smiled wearily. "History will judge," he said. He is hardly eating anything, and the skin is loose on his bony hands. I don't know what to do. I so much wish Michel was here. But at least Gonsalvo and his wife come often to see my uncle, so I know he is looked after.

1st October 1508

A letter from Mama came today. In Spain, too, people are afraid of an attack from Henry – though they are more afraid of the French. For the first time, Mama chides me for having fallen in love with a Frenchman. Couldn't I have found a nice Spaniard, she asks? But Michel has not been in France for years – he is a man of all nations. How I hate this wrangling and distrust.

Mama says Juana is now a prisoner, locked up by her father. Nobody knows if she is truly insane, but Ferdinand is ruling in her place, and he is making sure to keep her away from the public eye.

12th October 1508

Oh, what a rumpus! Catherine found out this morning that Fuensalida has been sending the plate, jewels and money that were meant to pay the last of her dowry out of the country "for safe keeping" in the Netherlands, because he is so sure there will be war between England and Spain. This all emerged when he walked into her room this morning and told her she must not go to the ceremony of Mary's betrothal.

Mary, Harry's little sister, is thirteen now, and when Philip and Juana came here because of the storm, she was promised to their son Charles. Catherine is very fond of Mary, and she was outraged by Fuensalida's high-handed order. It would be an unthinkable insult to Henry and the whole royal family to stay away from the ceremony. Catherine shouted at the ambassador, telling him he had no idea of manners or courtesy and was totally unfitted to be a diplomat. (In which I agree with her.) He tried to stand his ground, but she jumped to her feet and snatched up her embroidery scissors, and I think he really believed she might attack him. Anyway, he fled, and Catherine went rampaging to the King.

13th October 1508

When Fuensalida rode into Court this morning, the King's servants simply took his horse by the bridle and turned it round, directing the ambassador out again. Henry has refused to see him any more.

I sent a note to Uncle Rod, telling him of this in hopes it would cheer him up.

15th October 1508

The messenger who took my note brought no reply. He said my uncle seemed listless and ill. Catherine caught me weeping and asked what was the matter, and I told her. She promises she will send her own doctor to him. I hope it may do some good.

3rd November 1508

A short letter came from Uncle Rod today, written in his own hand, for which I thank God. I must not worry about him, he says. Gonsalvo or Bianca come every day, sometimes with their little son Miguel, and his landlady is kind. As to death, he says, that is not a thing to be feared. It is only a return to the mystery in which we existed before we were born. At the end he added a guarded sentence. "Gonsalvo will say for me that which should be said." He means *kaddish*, the Jewish prayer for the dead. Tears come to my eyes at that, but I am not sure why.

20th December 1508

Mary's betrothal has been celebrated with the usual splendour. Though still only thirteen, she was wonderfully composed, and a long account of the whole ceremony has been written in Latin, to be widely circulated. A translation in Spanish is to go to King Ferdinand. As Michel might say, with a straight face, "I'm sure he'll love it."

And now we are to have another merry Christmas.

16th April 1509

King Henry is gravely ill. Here at Richmond, the palace which he designed and built, he fights for each laboured breath. The doctors are with him constantly, but I fear he is beyond the help of their leeches and potions. The court is hushed, and there is a constant murmur of prayer.

Nobody prays for my old uncle, who also lies waiting for his death, though in complete tranquillity. A message came from Gonsalvo yesterday, to say I should come if I wished to see him still alive, and Catherine said I must go at once. I don't know how she arranged it, but I was taken that morning by boat down the river to the Strand, with a manservant to look after me.

It seemed strange that the spirit still inhabited Uncle Rod's bony frame, so wasted and fleshless has he become, but he smiled when he saw me. I had to bend close to hear what he was trying to say. "There is nothing to do." It was just a whisper, then he closed his eyes in great tiredness. I still wonder what he meant. A life's work completed, perhaps, and the last ends tied up. Or maybe he was thinking of the wreckage that had been made of his skilled care, and the braggart non-diplomacy that had replaced it. Nothing to be done. The nations are heading for war.

17th April 1509

I wish I had not come back to Richmond last night. I should have sent the man back alone. I should have stayed. Uncle Rod died at dawn this morning, and I was not there. Gonsalvo sent a rider to Richmond with a letter to tell me what had happened. I cannot stop weeping.

21st April 1509

Henry VII of England is dead.

Such a public death. Not for him the obscurity of a small bedroom in a street near the river – Henry died with statesmen round his bed and the royal coat of arms above him. I felt bitter at first, but this evening I know I would not have wanted Uncle Rod to have been subjected to such a blaze of morbid interest. He died as he would have wished, with his son beside him and the murmured chant of an ancient prayer in his ears.

Henry, too, was watched over by his son in the slow days of his dying. Young Harry was with him constantly – but not just out of compassion. Together, the son and the dying father agreed on how the kingship should continue, and how England should stand among the other nations.

I knew nothing of this, of course, until Catherine, fresh from a meeting with Prince Harry, burst into the room where I was mending a dress yet again, and seized my hands, whirling me into a dance. "Eva! Do you know what the King's last words were? He said Harry and I must wed! We must marry before the coronation, so the people will have a new king and his queen. I have won, Eva! I've won, I've won!"

It's hard to believe, but it seems to be true. We can hardly celebrate when the King's body lies in state, awaiting burial, but all the Spaniards here are in a state of suppressed excitement. And Catherine herself seems to radiate pure joy.

11th May 1509

Yesterday was the King's funeral. Five black horses drew his carriage through black-shrouded streets. And Harry, or Henry, as I suppose I should now call him – Henry VIII of England – will marry Catherine in a month's time at the Church of the Observant Friars, by Greenwich Palace – the place where he was christened eighteen years ago.

Fuensalida is utterly confounded. He could not believe it when young Henry told him of his father's death-bed instruction. He walks about in silent consternation, like a man whose world has fallen about his ears, and he will have to retrieve all the money and valuables he spirited away to Flanders. "Everybody makes mistakes," Henry told him kindly when he gave this instruction. But the corners of his mouth twitched, and everyone saw his amusement. Henry is not to be trifled with, though. Catherine told me in a private moment this evening that he has already made arrangements for Fuensalida to be returned to Spain.

3rd June 1509

When will I get time to write a proper entry again? There is such a frenzy of cutting and stitching that I never have a free moment. Catherine's little household has to leap from obscurity to a queen's opulence, and we are so taken by surprise that we hardly know where to start. Lady Margaret Beaufort, who is regent of the country during this time between kings, has helped us by making her own stocks of silks and velvets available and by lending us sempstresses and embroidresses. Luckily the daylight is long at this time of the year, for some of the detailed work is hard to do by the glow of candles. We work at such a rate that it's a kind of madness, but as Michel said once, it's better to be mad than dull. Nobody could call it dull here now. Not any more.

24th June 1509 Midsummer Day

At last! Henry VIII of England and Catherine, Princess of Aragon and Wales (I feel I must give them their full titles) were crowned King and Queen of England today after their private marriage yesterday in Greenwich. They spent the night at the Tower of London, as tradition demands, and the waiting crowds yelled and cheered when they saw them. Henry looked magnificent, so tall and broad, every inch a king, clad in richly embroidered cloth of gold and his hair a red-gold colour too. Catherine rode in a white silk litter carried between two white palfreys, looking as young and untouched by the years as she was when she went to that other wedding. It seems now to have been so brief and so long ago that it might never have happened, except that these eight years of hardship and insult have been its direct result.

The people in the streets didn't care. For them, Catherine was their beautiful new bride-queen, and they roared their approval of her all the way to Westminster Abbey. We, her ladies, rode beside her on white horses, and our robes of blue velvet, edged with crimson, set off her silken whiteness perfectly. The streets were hung with scarlet cloth, thousands of yards of it, and the entire court was dressed in scarlet robes, richly furred. For weeks, Lady Margaret has been buying up all the cloth she could lay her hands on. What an amazing woman she is! At 66 years old, she has run the country since her son's death, and now she presides over the wedding and coronation of her grandson as well, with absolute efficiency. No wonder she looks exhausted.

When the procession had entered the Abbey, no one could hold the crowds back. They fell upon the white damask cloth that had lined the way in and hacked it to pieces, grabbing and snatching at scraps of it to take home in an almost religious frenzy, as though the tattered bits of silk they clutched were an actual part of royalty. But their avidness made me think of crows tearing at a dead lamb, and I found them frightening. Perhaps they frighten kings as well, which is why they like to show their wealth and power. And why any real trouble-maker is promptly hanged.

27th June 1509

The feasting goes on and on, in joyous celebration – and there is a sense of relief, too, as though we have all escaped from a crabbed hand that kept us from happiness. There is a new gaiety about the jousting and carnival, a new sense of youth and high spirits. Energy seems to radiate from Henry, who is free at last from that stuffy room with no door except the one into his father's chamber. He is laughing and tireless, charging across the tiltyard on the great stallion he rides, banqueting and dancing – but all the time his eyes seek Catherine's in an intimacy that almost makes me blush, and he constantly returns to her side to run his hand down her back and touch his lips to hers. She is his first love, and he cannot get enough of her.

Catherine matches him perfectly. She shares his joy in music and dancing, revels as he does in new clothes and the glory of jewels and rich embroideries, and yesterday she was out with him on a hunting expedition, strong and graceful on her white horse, a hawk on her wrist, truly the warrior queen's daughter. But she has learned much in these hard years, and she has a composure about her which compels her young husband's admiration. She is no longer a girl; she has become a graceful, wise young woman. She has had eight years to think about becoming Henry's queen, and now that it has come about, she is performing her new role faultlessly.

29th June 1509

Alas, Lady Margaret Beaufort died this afternoon, quite suddenly. She retired to her room after supervising yet another sumptuous meal of roast swan and fine wines, and fell into eternal sleep. Her death grieves me more than any I have known save that of Uncle Rod. Henry wept in Catherine's arms when he was told the news, though he quickly gathered his dignity as he had to. He is the king, even though he throws himself into his games of hunting and music and mock-war with a boy's intensity.

At least Lady Margaret lived to see the despatch brought by an envoy from Scotland this morning. A treaty of peace has been signed between England and Scotland, thank God, and the letter from King James that came with it was full of warm congratulations on Henry's marriage and coronation. Dare I hope these brothers-in-law will at last learn to trust each other?

Doubts nag at my mind. Henry announced the treaty as a triumph, and I am sure he is relieved to know that Scotland will not attack from the north should he go to war with France, but somehow I can see Uncle Rod shaking his head.

3rd July 1509

As one might expect, Lady Margaret left a careful, detailed will. Her library of glorious books is to go to the college she founded in Cambridge, though Henry has been given some of the best of them. He is the head of the family now, so he inherits the bulk of her estate, but she shared her jewellery between the royal grand-daughters and Catherine. A secret came to light, too. When Arthur died, his possessions were shared among the family, but because Margaret was due to marry James and go to Scotland, her bequest of gold and jewels and plate was kept in trust for her, and she has never yet received it.

Henry's expression did not change when this was read out, but I thought it was rather disgraceful. Uncle Rod left me some books, which I treasure, but how would I have felt if Gonsalvo had refused to give them to me? Such a thing never crossed my mind, of course – or his. He had the books carefully packed and sent to me only a week later. But the property of royal families is different. It represents bargaining power, and I suppose the old King could not bear the idea of such valuable stuff going to Scotland, a country that was always a potential enemy. As so often, I feel sorry for Margaret – but at least she is genuinely happy in her marriage. Catherine says her letters always speak with pride and affection of her Scottish husband, whom she obviously adores. Perhaps my pity is misplaced, and I should envy her.

22nd July 1509

Michel is here! No creeping through the back door this time – he has come as the court jester with a delegation from Prince Charles, Philip's son, the boy who will marry Mary.

I have hardly managed to see him. There was the inevitable banquet tonight, and Michel was joking and clowning. Henry laughed so much that he spluttered wine all over his gold-embroidered doublet – messy man – but he gave Michel six pounds at the end of the evening, and summoned him to his private chambers, that he and the Queen might have some further amusement. Sometimes I curse Henry's inexhaustible energy.

23rd July 1509

Dear Lord, I give thanks for this day! Early this morning, I heard a tune being whistled in the garden, and jumped up to look out. There was Michel, standing on the grass all silver with dew, smiling up at me. He held out his hands, and I said, "Wait." I ran down just as I was, in my nightdress, with my feet bare and my hair loose. And he dropped to one knee, laughing and yet serious, and … asked me to be his wife.

When I could catch her alone I told Catherine, and she kissed me and wished me well. There was a time when we would have hugged each other, but she is the queen now, and even I, her childhood friend, have to remember that. But she still loves me, and promised she would tell Henry and ask him to do what he could for us. She kept her word, for he summoned Michel and me to go and see him in his private chamber. We did not know what to expect, but he seemed amused and gave us his blessing. Then he said the Queen did not want to lose me, and for a moment my heart lurched in panic, lest I should be forced to stay in London when Michel goes back to the Netherlands. But Henry smiled, looking very pleased with himself. He had arranged an exchange of fools, he said. Michel would stay here and in his place John Scot would go back to young Charles. John Scot is a dwarf who came here with the party that returned from escorting Margaret to her wedding in Edinburgh, and I have never much liked him. Perhaps Henry feels likewise, because he grinned and said he had the best of the bargain.

Michel turned at the door to doff his cap with a courtly bow, and managed to get the feather stuck between his knees. I tugged at his arm, fearing he had gone too far, but Henry roared with laughter. Michel says clowning is always about going too far. That's why it's funny, he says. You live on the edge of disaster, but just avoid it.

Don Alessandro will marry us in September. I am so happy that I can hardly breathe.

21st September 1509

I have hardly thought about writing my diary. With Michel here, I am not lonely, so I haven't felt the same need to use the blank pages as a substitute for someone to talk to. And on the best day of my life I was too busy living it to think of writing about it. We were married here in the chapel at Windsor, and Catherine came, together with dozens of courtiers both English and Spanish. There was a feast afterwards, followed by music and dancing, and for us there was no embarrassing ritual of bishops and blessings. Our first night as a married couple was private to us.

Catherine gave me a delicate gold pendant set with a diamond and small sapphires and, as a better present still, whispered her secret in my ear. She is with child! I hug the knowledge as an added delight in that glorious day, even though everyone knows it now.

I pray that Catherine's baby will live and be healthy. Michel says the newborn sons and daughters of queens take one look at the world, realize they are royal and promptly die. Who can blame them, he says? I should not laugh, but I do. My life is full of laughter now.

14th November 1509

News has just reached us from Scotland that Margaret has given birth to a son. The child seems healthy, and he is to be called Arthur, in memory of Margaret's brother. Perhaps Margaret has been thinking of the bequest Arthur left her, and hopes this gentle hint may nudge Henry towards sending it. "She'll be lucky," Michel says. And he's probably right.

30th January 1510

Catherine has given birth before her due time, to a little girl who was dead when she came into the world. All over the court, I hear people say, "At least it was a girl", trying to console themselves. The loss of a son would have been so much worse. I went to see Catherine this evening. She is not seriously ill, thank God, but she is white-faced and wretched, and I could not find words to comfort her. We both know child-birth is a dangerous business – but at least she herself is alive. So many women die.

I could not bring myself to tell her that I am myself pregnant. To tell the truth, it frightens me a little, but Michel reminds me of what he said about royal children. Our baby will not be burdened with the hopes of nations, so it will be carefree and healthy.

It may not be merely the hopes of nations that cast such a blight on the Tudor women's attempts to produce heirs. I have heard that an illness runs through the royal line, transmitted to their wives and affecting their unborn children, causing them to die in the womb or be born sickly and short-lived. Nobody says this aloud, but the rumour runs underground like the roots of sorrel, popping up in a new growth of gossip and head-shaking every time a royal child fails to live. I must not listen, in case my own baby is affected by the very idea. In any case, I'll be too busy for idle talk. I have to make little clothes and caps and shawls as well as keep up with my work at court.

Catherine has entrusted me with the supervision of all the embroidery done by her staff of needlewomen, and while I am flattered, and pleased to have the money it brings, the next months are going to be frantically busy.

16th August 1510

Three days ago my daughter was born. She is pink and beautiful, and her name is Rosanna, Rose for her pinkness and health, and Anna because it is my mother's name. I have sent a letter to Mama with the news. How I wish she could be here!

Michel is so proud of his daughter. He cradles her lovingly, offering his finger to the grip of her little hand. Her birth was a long, agonizing struggle, but all that is easily forgotten in the joy of her living presence. Daily I thank God for her.

17th August 1510

As if to underline my good fortune, a messenger from Scotland today brought the news that Margaret's little son, Arthur, has died. This is the third child she has lost. Michel remarked that Henry will be pleased. "That leaves the field open for him and Catherine," he said. A cynical observation, but perhaps it is true. Catherine is pregnant again, and the whole court is praying for her.

12th October 1510

We have a new ambassador, a replacement for Fuensalida. This one, too, is a strutting popinjay, but it doesn't matter much. Henry turns to Catherine whenever he needs guidance, and she is always ready with a quiet word of advice or the supply of a needed fact.

She amazes me now. I'd never have thought she could play so many parts, all of them with such grace and self-assurance. Henry is still a boy at heart – perhaps some boyhood is owed to him after the years of being confined by his careful father – and he loves to play games. Sometimes he and his friends dress up as Robin Hood and his outlaws, or as Moors with black faces, or booted Russians, and come bursting into the room where Catherine and her ladies are sitting, as if to take us prisoner. Catherine always jumps up and shrieks with just the right mixture of delight and theatrical terror, joining in his game because she loves him and because he is her king.

At other times she is very much the diplomat. Henry has been worrying about Ferdinand having taken a French wife and (worse) having signed a peace pact with France, but Catherine looked at him calmly with her grey eyes. "My lord," she said respectfully, "you are a great statesman; you will understand my father's motives. In his place, threatened by attack from France, would you not play for time? Make a marriage, sign a pact, buy a few months of safety? If you wish it, he will be on your side when the time comes. Believe me." And he had no choice but to smile down at her – she comes barely to his shoulder – then take her in his arms and call her his clever little vixen.

Even Catherine can't always restrain Henry, though. He's like a young bull let out of his shed in the spring, Michel says, ready to charge at anything that catches his eye. He loves the idea of war. To him it means honour and glory, a chance to be thought of with the same respect as that earlier Henry, Henry V, who beat the French at Agincourt. He is so full of this idea that such things as tact and carefulness are often forgotten. At a meeting with the French ambassador last week, he quite forgot that Catherine had advised him to follow her father's example and sign a temporary peace treaty. When this was suggested, he blew up instantly and roared, "*I* ask for peace with France? Who dares say so?" The tale has run round the court with much delighted gossip about how Catherine had to call for an adjournment and some wine while she calmed her husband down and made him see sense.

She has succeeded in bringing Henry and her father together, at least for the purpose of this proposed war. Ferdinand has reminded Henry that the area surrounding the French city of Bordeaux used to be under English rule until about 60 years ago. Its citizens, he says, are longing to have Henry as their king. Michel snorted with laughter when he heard this, and said the French would rather be ruled by a pig than by Henry. (That, of course, is strictly between ourselves.) Meanwhile, Catherine expects her next baby in January, and Henry is pleased with himself. God willing, he will become a father and the liberator of the suffering people of France. Or so he hopes.

1st January 1511

There could not be a better start to this new year. Catherine has given birth to a boy, and all the church bells are ringing. The court has gone into instant rejoicing, and Henry is cock-a-hoop with pride. The child will be called after him, of course, another Henry to come to the throne in his turn, and all London knows a royal prince has been born. Bonfires burn in the streets and cannon are booming from the Tower.

Nobody seems to take much notice of Catherine in all this, but I am so happy for her, knowing as I do the delight of a living baby. Sometimes Michel picks

Rosanna up by her little feet and holds her upside down in the air. I was horrified the first time he did it, but he says she may as well get used to the idea that the world is topsy turvy. And she seems to love it, crowing and gurgling with delight. I am making a new cap for her, sewn with tiny blue beads and satin ribbon.

21st February 1511

The celebrations were short-lived, as was the little prince. He died early this morning after barely seven weeks of quiet, sickly life. Catherine is distraught, and Henry walks about with an ashen face. This is the greatest blow he has ever suffered, and he has no way to combat it.

4th June 1511

Busy, busy, busy. Constant embroidery work for the court, and supervising all the other needlewomen as well. Michel says I am doing too much – looking after him and Rosanna is enough. Perhaps he is right. For a while, I thought I was pregnant again, but it came to nothing. I grieve a little for a child that might have been, even if it existed only in my imagination.

Henry's preparations for war continue. They seem to be some consolation to him for his lost son, but Catherine looks older, and has lost much of her happiness.

12th March 1512

I still have little time to write – or inclination, in fact. The days go by so fast, and Rosanna is walking now.

Not just walking, but climbing and scrambling and getting into everything. She babbles in a mixture of English and Spanish, for I have always spoken to her in my own language, and she even knows a few French words as well, from Michel. This delights him, but it would be rash to speak French outside the safety of our own quarters. War fever is mounting, and the Pope has called on all the rulers of Europe to join in what he calls the Holy League against France. The Pope hates Louis because he was rash enough to criticize the Pope for having fathered so many illegitimate children. I cannot help feeling that these war games are a personal sport between men of power. Henry has bought 48 immense guns, each one over seven feet long, and has given them names and badges, as if they were living things.

17th March 1512

King James of Scotland has written to all the kings of Europe, calling for peace. We are all Christians, he says, and should learn to tolerate each other. I think he is right, but Catherine is contemptuous. She says James has no right to call himself a peacekeeper. "Look how often he has raided England's northern border," she says.

Michel has a great respect for James. Court jesters know more than most people about what goes on in high circles, and they gossip among themselves constantly, of course, passing on any bits of scandalous news and scraps of inside information. Knowing what is happening is all part of their job. Those of them who know James all like him. He's a thoughtful man, they say, practical and yet imaginative, and he adores his wife even though he was so wild as a young man. Margaret expects another baby very soon. Michel says he sometimes wishes we were at the Scottish court instead of this one, but yesterday he added that it couldn't be as ridiculous as the English one. "This lot fancy themselves so important that they're half off their heads," he said. "Fascinated with themselves. Quite absurd. And what would a jester do without absurdity? I'd be no good with James – he's much too sensible."

Henry would be outraged. He likes to think of himself as extremely sensible. He spends a lot of time with Wolsey now, and is beginning to value his opinion more than Catherine's. Wolsey is what Michel calls "one of the New Men". His father was a butcher in Ipswich, and he climbed out of the blood and sawdust through sheer cleverness. Henry is a New Man, too, I suppose, unlike James, who comes of the ancient Stuart line. He looks ahead to a grand future, and picks his friends accordingly. Wolsey is the only cleric I know who wears robes made from pure, heavy silk.

28th April 1512

Margaret's baby was born on the 10th of this month, and it is a boy, healthy and strong, the letter says. He, like his short-lived elder brother, will be called James. Perhaps Catherine and Henry, still childless, regret having sent her the Girdle of Our Lady, a most precious relic, reputed to work wonders for queens desiring the safe delivery of a child.

7th June 1512

Twelve thousand men have sailed for the Basque frontier between Spain and France, following 6,000 last week. Such numbers! They are under the command of the Marquess of Dorset, who seems to me a foppish gentleman for the business of war, but perhaps he will surprise us. And now we wait for news.

10th July 1512

Dorset's army waits at San Sebastian to be joined by the Spanish troops of Ferdinand. It must be terribly hot in that place between the mountains and the Bay of Biscay, and the English will not understand that one has to have a siesta in the afternoon. It's very unhealthy to be out in the blaze of midday. The French watch them and seem perplexed, the despatch says. No shot has yet been fired.

Catherine is frowning and puzzled. Her father should have met Dorset long before now, with cavalry troops and artillery as arranged. The English could not ship large numbers of horses, and they depend on Ferdinand to supply them with mounts. Something has gone wrong.

23rd July 1512

The court has begun to mutter that Ferdinand has betrayed Henry. Instead of meeting the English troops as he promised, he has gone straight to Navarre, where he is besieging that small kingdom, knowing the French will not come to its aid as they are still watching Dorset's army and waiting for it to make a move. But the English cannot move, for they still have no horses. They are sweltering in San Sebastian, bored and angry and drinking too much wine.

It's an embarrassing situation for Catherine. Her father it seems has deceived her as well as everyone else about his true intentions. Quite obviously, he has used the English troops to tie up the French while he, Ferdinand, gets on with taking Navarre. Catherine falls back on blaming the ambassador, Caroz, but he is as baffled as anyone else. And Henry, of course, is raging.

2nd September 1512

Another letter came from Dorset's army today, and its contents were soon common gossip. The men are on the point of mutiny. They are nearly all ill now, with a stomach sickness that has killed many of them. They blame the garlic! So stupid – but I can't help feeling sorry for them. Henry has sent a herald with a return message, telling Dorset the army must stay where it is for the winter, ready for a fresh campaign in the spring. "You see what I mean?" Michel said. "Totally absurd. They'll all be dead."

29th September 1512

Henry's herald was shouted down. The soldiers would not listen, and their yells turned into a chant of "Home! Home! Home!" Henry will have to give in.

11th December 1512

The wretched stragglers who were once an army have come home. And Ferdinand has sent an incredibly insulting message, saying the English troops were of such poor quality that he couldn't use them. He adds that he has had to make peace with the French for six months, for fear they might invade England, having seen how hopeless the English soldiers are.

Henry is gibbering with rage. He was all for hanging the Marquess of Dorset the moment he set foot in England, but Catherine managed to dissuade him. It would do his reputation no good, she said. Better by far to show the watching world that England is still a nation to be feared. He must prepare for war next year. And this time, he must win.

20th December 1512

James of Scotland is still trying to negotiate a peace between France and her enemies. He sent an envoy to Paris – or at least, he tried to, but Henry turned the man back at the border. It's hardly surprising, Michel says. Henry knows a French ship arrived at the Leith docks two weeks ago laden with wine and cloth of gold, but also with artillery guns of a new and very accurate kind, together with 300 cannon balls and a large quantity of gunpowder.

13th January 1513

Henry was in a fresh storm of rage this morning. His spies in Scotland tell him that James has received a letter from the French queen, Anne of Brittany, with which she sends her glove and a turquoise ring, begging him to come to the aid of France when England and Spain attack her.

"She sent him her *glove*," Michel said, exhausted after the hard work of restoring the King to something like good humour. "You know what that means. It is the traditional sign given to a knight by a lady in distress. Chivalry will not allow him to ignore it."

Henry is infuriated that his brother-in-law takes up this high moral tone – "Posing," he bellowed, "as the saintly peace-keeper of Europe!" Henry hates peace. Enemies are a necessary and enjoyable evil, part of the great game of war, but peace is the ultimate wet-blanket, undoing the game itself. We all breathed more easily when he went storming out to the river, there to be ferried down to Woolwich, to inspect the progress of his new ships that are being built. Whole forests have been cut down for the sake of this armada, and the sky seems strangely open and empty where the great oaks used to stand. But Henry loves his ships, specially the huge flagship, the *Great Harry*. Suits of armour arrive daily from Italy and Spain, together with hundreds of fine new swords and daggers, and he has twelve immense cannon, sent by Maximilian, which he calls *The Twelve Apostles*.

Both Catherine and Mary have received letters from Margaret in Scotland. She had a miscarriage in the autumn, and was ill for some time, and in recent weeks she has been much troubled by nightmares. She dreams constantly of her husband's death, and of standing alone on a high cliff in a desolate place, with the sea crashing on rocks a long way below her. She always sends loving wishes to Henry in her letters, but I doubt whether he writes back to her. Scotland, too, is part of the great game of war, and to see it through the eyes of his sister would be dangerously close to wishing for peace.

4th May 1513

Henry is deeply perturbed about the Queen of France's appeal to James. He has sent an envoy to Scotland – Nicholas West, the dry, virtuous Dean of Windsor – hoping to get a promise from James that he will not aid France in the coming war.

12th May 1513

West has returned, ruffled and angry, and the court is full of excited gossip, as usual. They try to pump Michel, who is closer to the King than any of them, but he tells them he is just the pet monkey, and hops and gibbers until they shrug and turn away. I know, as they do not, how much Henry confides in him, and what a strain it is to be called upon to find crumbs of comfort and amusement in a morass of bad news. West utterly failed to bribe James to stay on the English side. He failed, too, in a clumsy attempt to bribe Margaret, offering her the gold and jewels bequeathed to her by Arthur in return for a promise that she would persuade James not to help France. Margaret simply laughed and walked out, for which I admire her, and after that she removed herself and her small son, James, to the castle of Linlithgow. She is pregnant again, expecting a baby in the autumn, and I would hate to be in her situation, caught between two sides in the war which will now undoubtedly come soon.

30th June 1513

It has started. Henry and his great fleet have set sail, complete with all their guns and armour, banners, lances, provisions and horses (for he is taking his own cavalry this time). My fingers are sore from stitching, since this war is also a travelling pageant of Tudor glory. Every tunic and jerkin and cloak, every saddle-cloth and even every tent has been gold-embroidered, and the army set off under a moving forest of plumes and banners. We have used bale upon bale of cloth of gold, both red and white, and tissue of silver, as well as silks and velvets in crimson and blue and purple, and countless yards of green and white cloth have gone into the making of tents and covers for waggons. The armourers and smiths have been working equally hard, engraving designs of antelopes and swans on to breastplates and forging silver medallions for harnesses and little gold bells to tinkle on bridles. This is the greatest tournament of Henry's life, and he has revelled in every moment of it.

Catherine, too, has thrown herself into it all. She rode to Dover with Henry at the head of the long procession, and at the sea's edge he proclaimed her Governor of the Realm in his absence, and put her in charge of northern defences. I did not go, for I am certainly pregnant again now, and it is making me often sick. Catherine agreed that I could stay at home when Michel spoke to her on my behalf. I felt ashamed to do so, for Catherine herself is expecting a child, and I suspect that she must despise me for giving in to such weakness. She ignores her condition, just as her mother did, the battling Isabella. Those who came back say she made a fiery speech to the assembled men. I can imagine how her Spanish-accented English rang out over the breaking of the waves.

And now they are gone. Henry insisted on taking Michel with him, and Rosanna does not understand where Papa has gone. God keep him safe.

29th July 1513

A messenger brought news today that Henry met as arranged with the Emperor Maximilian's army, under the walls of a French town called Thérouanne. It was pouring with rain. Such a shame, when the army had set out looking so glorious in its red and gold and Tudor-green. And Maximilian's men were all in black. It must have amused Michel – Henry's troops decked out in magnificence while the old Habsburg bandit sticks to practicalities. He does not play at war; it is his business.

In Henry's absence, Catherine has at once set about the business of running the country. I realize now what a soldier she is by instinct, for the first thing she did was to send a large army northwards, to cover the

Scottish border against attack. She intends to raise a second army of new recruits, to reinforce the first, which is under the command of the Earl of Surrey. "If James attacks, he will get his fingers burned," she said to me this evening. "And serve him right."

2nd September 1513

I pray for Michel's safety. Perhaps he is not in too much danger, for Henry's war seems to be little more than a glorified tournament. A few villages have been sacked and burned, but King Louis is mainly concerned with holding his advances in Italy, and has told his commanders merely to watch the English rather than engage with them. (Catherine receives daily despatches from Henry.) There has only been one skirmish so far, which ended in a spirited English chase after fleeing French cavalry. It sounds as if the whole campaign is, by Henry's standards, thoroughly enjoyable. All of us here are far more concerned with Scotland.

Margaret's last letter to her sister Mary spoke of continuing nightmares. She dreamed of the high cliff again, but, horrifyingly, she saw James fall to his death – and the diamonds in her jewel box had all turned to pearls, the emblems of widowhood. I never knew this was the meaning of pearls. We sewed so many of them into Catherine's veil for her first wedding to Arthur – and she was indeed a widow within a few months.

4th September 1513

Catherine's instincts were right. James has declared war on England. Everyone here is appalled, but Catherine is filled with energy and excitement. Her new troops are arriving by the hour, some of them from as far away as Wales and Cornwall, and she plans to ride with them herself for at least part of the way. I tried to tell her she should not do this. She carries a royal child within her, and strenuous days on the road could have a disastrous result. Both of us know that Isabella had several miscarriages because of taking part in warlike expeditions – but perhaps Catherine feels she can do no less. Michel would shake his head wearily. *Madness, madness.* I miss him so much.

8th September 1513

Catherine has set off for Buckingham at the head of her army. Wolsey's spies in the north reported that a group of wild Highlanders from the north of Scotland have already launched an attack, not waiting for King James, but they were quickly repulsed. James has gone to Linlithgow to say goodbye to Margaret.

12th September 1513

I can hardly bring myself to write about what has happened. I am shaken and sick at the thought of it, and glad in a way that this is almost the last page of my diary. I shall never keep another. Were it not for a kind of loyalty to Catherine, I would like to leave this court and live with Michel and our children as ordinary people do, knowing nothing of the great games of kings.

The Scottish army is utterly destroyed, and James is dead. Surrey met them in the Cheviot hills, at a place called Flodden. The Scots were tired from long marching, Wolsey's rider reports, and they had run short of food and ale. James made the mistake of ordering them to move the guns further up the ridge to a better position, but Surrey had plenty of time to deploy his troops, almost surrounding the Scots.

In three hours of fighting, 10,000 Scottish soldiers were killed. Ten *thousand*. There can hardly be an able-bodied man left in the country. The officers and nobility, too, were mown down, and at last James himself fell.

Catherine is still on her way to Buckingham, but her army will not be needed. This war, at least, is finished.

23rd September 1513

Catherine's expedition cost her dearly. On the night after her return, she lost the baby she had been expecting. Poor little future child – such an innocent casualty of war, and so deliberately put at risk, it seems to me. Catherine herself looks white-faced and exhausted, but she gave herself no rest after the miscarriage, and it has not stopped her from the grim business in which she is still taking part.

When she heard of James's death she ordered his body to be brought to London. I was with her when the captain of the travel-weary men came to report that this had been done. She went out with him, and bade me follow. I could not look at the wrapped and already stinking burden they carried, but she seemed exultant. The body must be taken to Henry in France, she said, that he might see for himself that the Scots had been vanquished.

An uneasy glance ran between the men, and their captain begged Catherine to excuse them from such a task. She looked at him with contempt, and turned on her heel.

Upstairs, she unwrapped the bundle of soiled clothing which the captain had given her, and held up a surcoat, gold-embroidered with the lion of Scotland. It was soaked with blood and slashed almost to ribbons. The captain had explained apologetically that after the battle the English troops had plundered the dead men who lay everywhere, stripping them of clothes and valuables. The body of the Scottish king, too, had been stripped, but the captain had managed to retrieve his coat. And as I watched her, sickened, Catherine smiled. "If I cannot send his dead enemy's body, Harry shall at least have his coat," she said. And in the afternoon of that same day, she despatched it to France.

28th September 1513

Michel is home, thank God, laughing about what he calls "Harry's summer circus". The real war was Catherine's, and it is Flodden that makes Europe's kings look with new respect at English fighting power.

Catherine spoke to me today of Margaret, whose child will be born with no father. Her little son, only eighteen months old, has been crowned James V of Scotland, but Margaret herself will rule as best she can over a country made derelict by the loss of its men. "I have sent people to comfort her," Catherine said. All her exultation had gone, and she looked drained of energy, her grey eyes shadowed with tiredness and distress. "Between us, Margaret and I must agree to keep the peace," she went on. "I am disbanding my army."

Her voice quavered a little, and she suddenly turned to me and wept. We were both aware that James, her brother-in-law, lies in the chapel here at Richmond, washed and embalmed and decently shrouded. The mute dignity of his dead presence makes it pitifully clear what Margaret has lost and what thousands of women have lost – 1,500 of them in England as well as the countless multitude in Scotland.

Catherine and I stood close, with our arms about each other as we have not done in many years. I knew she must be aware of the thickness of my body that is the coming baby, and ached with pity for her though I could say nothing about her own loss. After a few minutes she parted herself from me gently and wiped her eyes, then managed to smile. "Dear Eva," she said. "I hope the future will be kind to you."

With all my heart, I wish the same for Catherine. Proud, reckless, careful Catherine, my friend, my queen. May God guard her in what is to come.

Historical Note

Catherine of Aragon and Henry were married just before Henry was crowned King of England in 1509. Their marriage lasted for nearly 20 years, and it seems that it was a happy one, at least at the beginning, even though the reasons for it were political and not romantic. After he married Catherine, Henry is reported to have said, "If I were still free, I would still choose her for wife above all others."

The marriage of Henry's sister Margaret to the Scottish king James IV had also taken place for political reasons: Scotland had a history of alliance with England's greatest enemy, France, and the marriage came a year after a peace treaty between Scotland and England. But not long after Henry VIII came to the throne, James tried to break the peace with England, despite being married to Henry's sister. While Henry was away in France, Catherine was left in charge of the country and it was under her rule that the English army beat the Scots at the Battle of Flodden. The victorious Catherine really did send the blood-stained coat of the dead James IV to Henry, as Eva reports in her diary. Later, in 1542, Henry's English army was to defeat the army of Henry's own nephew – Margaret's son, James V of Scotland. In 1514, Henry's younger sister Mary was married to Louis XII of France, another political royal marriage.

Catherine gave birth to five children, but only one of them survived for more than a few weeks – a girl, Mary, not the hoped-for boy who could continue the Tudor line. By the time Catherine was in her thirties she was no longer able to have children and Henry wanted an end to the marriage. In 1527 he began to try and arrange a divorce, which proved extremely difficult and took six years to achieve. Before Henry could marry Catherine, back in 1509, he had needed special permission from the Pope, as head of the Catholic Church, because Catherine was his brother's widow. Now, Henry argued that the marriage should never have taken place and could be "annulled" – declared invalid. The Pope wouldn't give his permission – it would have meant going against the previous Pope's authority (who had allowed Catherine and Henry to marry in the first place), and secondly he needed to keep the peace with the powerful Emperor Charles V, who was Catherine of Aragon's nephew and who held most of Europe. Finally, Henry made himself head of the Church in England, and got his divorce without permission from the Pope. These must have been sad and humiliating years for Catherine: Henry went so far as to imprison their daughter, Mary, when she protested against the divorce. Henry's actions not only affected Catherine but the whole country – breaking away from the Pope's authority meant that Henry would go on to reform the Church in England, taking away land, wealth and power from the monasteries, and England would eventually become a Protestant country.

Catherine had been a popular queen with the people of England, but Henry's next wife, Anne Boleyn, was not. He married Anne in 1533 and she had a child the same year – another daughter, Elizabeth, which did not please Henry, who refused to go to the christening.

Catherine died in 1536 – there were rumours that she was poisoned, some said by Anne Boleyn, but there's no evidence to suggest that this was true. Henry showed no grief at her death.

Famously, Henry was married to six different wives, but none of them – apart from Catherine of Aragon – lasted for more than a few years. Anne Boleyn was executed in 1536, accused of treason. Henry married

Jane Seymour in the same year, who did provide him with the son he longed for but died soon after giving birth. His next three marriages, to Anne of Cleves, Catherine Howard and Catherine Parr, didn't produce any more children.

After his death in 1547, Henry's only son, Edward, became king at the age of nine, but died six years later. This meant that Mary, Catherine of Aragon's daughter with Henry, became queen. During her short reign she became known as Bloody Mary: she was fiercely Catholic, unlike her Protestant younger brother, and executed hundreds of Protestant "heretics". She died of influenza in 1558, leaving the throne to her half-sister Elizabeth (a Protestant), who would reign for 45 years before dying childless, the last of the Tudors.

Timeline of Tudor England

1485 Henry Tudor defeats Richard III at the Battle of Bosworth, and becomes Henry VII, the first Tudor king of England.

1486 Prince Arthur is born.

1491 Prince Henry (later Henry VIII) is born.

1501 Arthur marries Catherine of Aragon.

1502 Arthur dies.

1509 Henry VII dies. Prince Henry marries Catherine of Aragon and is crowned King Henry VIII.

1513 War with France and Scotland. James IV of Scotland dies at the Battle of Flodden Field.

1516 Catherine of Aragon has a daughter, Mary (later Queen Mary I).

1527 Henry starts his divorce from Catherine of Aragon.

1533 Henry marries Anne Boleyn. They have a daughter, Elizabeth (later Queen Elizabeth I).

1536 Anne Boleyn is beheaded. Henry marries Jane Seymour. Catherine of Aragon dies.

1536–9 The Reformation of the Church in England.

1537 Jane Seymour has a son, Edward (later Edward VI). She dies after the birth.

1540 Henry marries Anne of Cleves but they are divorced the same year. Henry marries Catherine Howard.

1542 Catherine Howard is beheaded.

1543 Henry marries Catherine Parr.

1547 Henry VIII dies. His only son becomes Edward VI of England.

1553 Edward VI dies. Catherine of Aragon's daughter, Mary, becomes Queen.

1554 Mary marries Philip of Spain.

1558 Mary dies. Elizabeth I becomes Queen of England.

1603 Elizabeth I, the last of the Tudor monarchs, dies.

Portrait, supposed to be of Catherine of Aragon, painted by Michiel Sittow in 1503/4.

Portrait of Henry VIII painted in the mid-1520s.

Stained glass portrait of Arthur, Prince of Wales, Catherine of Aragon's first husband. Arthur died in 1502 within a few months of his wedding. Catherine married his younger brother, Henry, in 1509.

A banquet in the Presence Chamber of Hampton Court Palace.

A view of Windsor Castle during the reign of Henry VIII's daughter, Elizabeth 1.

An engraving showing a picnic during a royal hunt in the sixteenth century.

A jester wearing a traditional costume with cap and bells.

Picture acknowledgments

P 159 (top)   Portrait of a woman, possibly Catherine of Aragon (1503/4), Michiel Sittow (1469-1525), Kunsthistorisches Museum, Vienna/Bridgeman Art Library

P 159 (bottom) Portrait of Henry VIII (c. 1525-30) English School (16th century) Philip Mould Historical Portraits Ltd, London/Bridgeman Art Library

P 160   Arthur, Prince of Wales, Mary Evans Picture Library

P 161   A banquet in the Presence Chamber, Hampton Court, Joseph Nash, *The Mansions of England in the Olden Time*, Mary Evans Picture Library

P 162   Windsor Castle, *Gentleman's Magazine*, Mary Evans Picture Library

P 163   Picnic during a royal hunt, from Turbervile's *The Noble Art of Venerie or Hunting*, Mary Evans Picture Library

P 164   Jester in cap and bells, A Kohl, Mary Evans Picture Library

My Story.

the hunger

The Diary of
Phyllis McCormack, Ireland 1845-1847

10th November, 1845

Horrible! Horrible! The rot has destroyed most of
the potatoes which were wholesome and sound when
we dug them out of the ground. Da opened up the
pit this morning and found it filled with nothing
but diseased mush. All we have left to eat are those
that hadn't yet gone underground.

"Six months provisions are a mass of stinking
rottenness. Where has it come from?" Da kept repeating
all morning. "Disease will take us all," he drawled.

My Story.

VOYAGE ON THE GREAT TITANIC

The Diary of Margaret Anne Brady, 1912

Monday 15th April, 1912

It was after midnight, and I could still hear people
moving about in the passageway. Before I had time to go
out and join them, there was a sharp knock on my door.

I opened it to see Robert. His eyes looked urgent.

"Good evening, Miss Brady," he said. "You need to
put on something warm, and report to the Boat Deck
with your life belt."

Miss Brady? When I heard that, I felt alarmed for
the first time. "A routine drill," he said. "No need to fret."

I knew he needed to get on with his duties,
so I found a smile for him and nodded...

"You'll not want to take your time, Margaret,"
he said in a very quiet voice.

It did not seem possible, but maybe this was not a drill.

My Story.

The Crystal Palace

The Diary of
Lily Hicks, London 1850-1851

17th April, 1850

The Crystal Palace is more wonderful every time we go, with coloured light everywhere, so airy and delicate, but strong. Not like a house, solid and heavy and shadowy, solid to the ground. Like being inside a diamond it is, or a fairy palace. Master has made a miracle, everybody says so. And as for the exhibits inside, there are more and more every day, 10,000 they say. We saw French and Belgian lace and English embroidery today, so fine the Queen can't have better – shawls and baby gowns and waistcoats, and Irish double damask tablecloths with shimmering ferns and flowers woven in. I was near crying with pure delight it was all so lovely.

My Story

BLITZ

The Diary of
Edie Benson, London 1940-1941

Friday 30th August, 1940

Last night was very still and clear. As Dad went
out for the evening shift, he looked up and said grimly,
"If they're ever going to come, it'll be on a night like this."
And sure enough, the first air-raid warning came at a
few minutes past nine. Mum was out at the ARP post,
and Shirl, Tom and I were huddled together in the
shelter with Chamberlain.

Shirl's teeth were chattering already. "Cor blimey!"
she said. "What's it going to be like in the middle
of winter? I've got no feeling in my toes at all."

I could see Tom was about to open his mouth and say
something clever when we heard the first explosion,
and then two more following close on the first one...

My Story.

TWENTIETH~ CENTURY GIRL

The Diary of
Flora Bonnington, London 1899-1900

22nd December, 1899

Time is marching forward, carrying us over the
threshold and pitching us, willy nilly, into a new
century. The prospect of growing up in that unexplored
territory is so thrilling that I fancy, if I close my
eyes tight, I can almost see the process taking place!
A day slips away like sand in a sand glass and then
another day dawns and so we are caught up in this
inevitable passage towards 1900. I bought a journal
and have begun to transfer all my scribblings of the last
few days into it. It will record my journey into the new
century. I shall call it "Twentieth-Century Girl",
for that is what I intend to be!